A Love Letter

A Love Letter

My Y Story, My Cancer Journey

By Mike Roberts

Printed in the United States

ISBN: 978-1-9399303-5-4

Library of Congress Control Number: 2014919122

This book is a work of fiction and in no way reflects the views or opinions of the LIVE**STRONG** Foundation, the YMCA of the USA or any local branch or association of the YMCA. The names, characters, places and incidents are products of the writer's imagination or have been used fictitiously and are not to be construed as real. Any resemblance to persons, living or dead, actual events, locales or organizations is entirely coincidental.

Published by

🌸 *Brandylane*

BRANDYLANE PUBLISHERS, INC.

brandylanepublishers.com

A Love Letter is dedicated to all cancer survivors, with a special thanks to the inspirational participants in our LIVE**STRONG** at the YMCA program. Love and respect to all the dedicated YMCA staff leading this effort around the country. Thanks to Marc Woods and Nick Teague for being good friends, the staff of the LIVE**STRONG** Foundation for all of their support, Carol Lazarus for her editing skills, Robert Pruett and Brandylane Publishers, and of course to my wife, Mary. Without her, I would not be in a position to do what I love to do.

Contents

Introduction

At age seventeen, Marc Woods lost his leg to cancer. He went on to win twelve medals in swimming at the Paralympic Games and is now a successful motivational speaker—and part-time mountain climber!

When I first met Mike Roberts, he was in his last year of college, and I was in my first. We'd meet socially and his enthusiasm for life was infectious. I'd lost a leg to cancer eighteen months earlier, but despite only being at college for a week or two, I was about to leave for the Paralympic Games in Seoul. "Bring back a gold!" he bellowed at me, giving me a hearty slap on the back. Thankfully, I didn't let him down, and I came back with five medals, including two golds.

Life has a habit of dropping challenges on us, challenges we'd not wish upon anyone and certainly not choose for ourselves. At college, I was the same as everyone else in so many ways; but in one big way, I was different. I had already faced a major challenge and had overcome it, whereas many of my friends had just taken their first steps out from under the protective umbrella of childhood.

Mike would be the first to admit that, at that time, he was untroubled by life's obstacles. Now, twenty-five years later, we are perhaps more equal in terms of our experiences. I have travelled the world attempting to help and inspire others both as an athlete and a speaker. Mike has done the same in his role as a YMCA professional in some particularly challenging settings, working in Kenya, Zimbabwe, the Dominican Republic, and Haiti. We both believe that exercise and sport can have a particularly positive impact on someone battling with cancer, and I am delighted to be able to support Mike's work in helping cancer survivors through the

LIVE**STRONG** at the YMCA program.

Writing a book is a challenge in itself, but I know Mike put his heart into this endeavor, and that's all any of us can really do. He has risen to the challenge, and you have the result of his success in your hands—now, please read and enjoy.

Marc Woods

Part One

~

Detroit, Tom Brady, and the YMCA

To LIVE**STRONG** at the YMCA staff and participants, 2010:

*"If it wasn't for you guys and LIVE**STRONG** at the YMCA, I would be a hermit. I would sit home alone all day in my own sorrow, thinking about how I had cancer. Now, I come to the downtown Y almost every day, even when we don't meet as a group. I am so thankful to have been connected with such wonderful people that are helping me become happier and healthier!"*

"Although we were all at different stages of our recovery, and we all had different goals, we were able to celebrate each other's accomplishments, no matter how big or small they were . . . , whether it was a new bench-press record, or just being able to walk up the stairs without stopping."

*"You know, there is a fear factor when you find out you have cancer. You don't want to admit that you have it. You feel ostracized. But you have to get out. And, when I come here, I feel welcomed. I think LIVE**STRONG** at the YMCA is a lifesaver."*

"Working at the Y gives me the unique opportunity—actually it's more of a unique responsibility—to wake up each morning and help people in their quest to live healthier, more fulfilling lives."

January 2012

1

Ethan Clarke was a forty-five-year-old accountant who had recently been diagnosed with cancer. When it was clear that a long, life-or-death journey lay ahead, he started writing, something he had not done since he was a young man with dreams and a love of words and wordplay. In hindsight, he should have started writing immediately, as he took his first step on this dark new path, because the self-discipline needed to choose words of meaning and the rhythm that came with typing were soothing. But at the time, as the word "cancer" appeared and hovered, his mind was elsewhere.

Ethan liked to write, but when he was told he had the disease, he did not think about things he liked—until the time came that he needed and sought companionship, and then putting words on paper felt like greeting an old friend. It was lyrical, poetic, factual, but it was also an outpouring of emotions that could help in his battle to stave off death. Whatever it was, it felt good, so Ethan made a pact with his fingers and mind to write about his experiences before the sun went down each day.

Friday was a good day, even for a person with cancer, and Ethan typed with end-of-the-week whimsy. On this Friday it felt good to be alive and in Clearwater, Florida. The highlight was an hour or so he spent sitting on a bench near the end of Pier 60, looking out at the sea, which was choppy but still a soothing Gulf of Mexico blue. The water churned as the waves tripped over the surface, pushed along by the Gulf breezes. At first, the pier was busy as he sat there, staring at the horizon. But when the wonders of the sunset were over, it became quiet. That was the nicest time: being alone, admiring the afterglow, and listening to the sounds of the sea and the air.

Ethan carried an iPad with him everywhere, so that he could jot down thoughts and feelings as they came to him. A long, long time ago, when he'd been in college, his first-ever job was as a part-time journalist at the *Detroit Free Press*. Ethan loved that job, loved to write about anything that they needed him to write about, from a feud at City Hall, to a sickly lion cub at the zoo, to the very bad boys at the Detroit Pistons. He was cheap and he was good, and the editor at that time, a very large Italian American whom they called Fat-Fingered Tony, liked all things good.

Ethan Clarke's family home was originally in Downriver, a smoky trail of gray, scarred communities that lined the river just south of Detroit. It was a gritty area, full of hard-working factories on a hard-working waterway, and populated by men and women who rose at dawn and fell into bed well past dusk, exhausted from toil. It was the place to be in its time, home to a new influx of Americans from the south and immigrant Americans from farther south and east and west. That was the time when Detroit ran the world with ease and acclaim, filled its highways and airways—until times changed.

Ethan had been young when he lived in Downriver, but he remembered walking the streets with his younger brother and feeling the gray around him. It wasn't the color gray, but rather a rough, metallic thing that he could taste on his tongue, a presence that came from old industry and lingered in the fog, making the way forward hard to see. He remembered riding his bike by the river, curving around ruts and potholes in the pavement, and looking down at water that mirrored a murky future for the city.

His father, Thomas, made a significant job switch in the seventies, and the family moved to Royal Oak, an affluent suburb of Detroit made for the even newer workers and families, an area with trees, grass, roads, and paths that were safe for feet and bikes. Still, there was a taste on Ethan's tongue, not industrial this time but emotional: a bitterness that grew stronger when his father left home. It turned out that the change of scenery had been an attempt to put a bandage on a wounded family full of angry boys and girls who wanted to be loved, not tolerated. The new house was gorgeous, with rooms everywhere, both above and below ground, but it soon began to echo without the things a home needed to fill its empty spaces.

Ethan went to college at the University of Detroit. The main campus was not far from his home and also not far from the downtown area of the city. He studied accounting at the business school and wrote for the school paper. An article he penned about the "phantom foul" that lost the Detroit Pistons game six of the NBA finals in 1988 caught the eye of a professor who knew a city councilman who knew the editor of the *Detroit Free Press*, and suddenly Ethan Clarke had the best part-time job he could have imagined.

He was not a gregarious person by nature, but journalism was a mask and writing a voice. Ethan drove an old 1950s Ford truck that his dad had left behind after he walked out, and he put most of his miles on it in the heart of the city as he trundled up and down Woodward and Michigan Avenue, talking to car dealers and police officers, to baseball fans and bums on the street. He may have grown up and gone to school in some tough parts of town, but there was something about Detroit that he loved. Every street, every corner, every chipped and graffiti-covered building had a hard luck/good luck story and hard luck/good luck people sitting or leaning close by who could tell that story. It was a black-and-white city with steam coming out of its manhole covers—steam that smelled of ambivalent sweat.

Tony gave his protégé assignments, but because he hardly paid him anything, he also let Ethan write whatever he wanted to write—and so hundreds of character-driven tales appeared, involving teenagers and old, rusty hoops, and grandmothers with no teeth but with words that could bite. There was one tale about a cursing, smoking, snowplow-driving Polish immigrant, and another about street hockey players with no shoes but with slap shots that sang. When he was a journalist, Ethan was a character himself, with wit and nerve and a notebook that allowed him to talk and listen and ask questions that evoked thought and thoughtful answers.

Most of these stories ended up in a file on Tony's desk, with prose that was laudable and infinitely readable, but not always printable—though some did make it onto page four or five of the paper. Ethan knew his editor liked him, thought he had potential, and liked the fact that he listened to his advice and his reminiscences.

Far from Michigan, the Gulf of Mexico was not Detroit, and notes made on a glowing screen instead of a pad of paper were unruffled by the wind and unblemished by crossing and scribbling. When it began to get dark, Ethan closed his eyes and listened to the sound of water slapping against the pier legs, seagulls calling, and pelican wings whispering, everything contrasting well with memories of that faraway city with its smoke and screams and sirens.

It had been two months since he'd sat in a doctor's office and heard words, spoken softly, that sounded like Detroit on a busy day:

"Adrenal cortical carcinoma is a very rare form of cancer that develops in the adrenal gland."

Adrenal cortical carcinoma. The words themselves were alien, invasive. It was an extremely aggressive cancer and was discovered because Ethan had started having pain in his stomach and felt full, bloated—even though he was eating less and less. When a scan revealed that he had a six-pound, football-sized tumor nestling next to his kidney, his appetite diminished even further.

There were a variety of treatment options for adrenal cancer, but for a tumor of that size, surgery was needed, and the procedure had lasted nine hours. When Ethan saw the tumor, and had recovered from the shock of seeing his ravager in all of its fluid, fleshy splendor, he'd pondered and fretted over the intricacies involved in removing a mass of that size without causing damage or leaving even the smallest trace of malignancy behind. Initially the operation seemed successful, but he had to wait for tests to make sure the cancer hadn't spread, and he had to take oral chemotherapy pills during the wait, as a precaution. Ethan felt he could be a patient person, but waiting without knowing, when the waiting meant life or death—well, that kind of waiting involved more than patience. It involved character and individuality and strength. And as he walked a dark, unfamiliar path, Ethan Clarke felt weak.

We all hope, and maybe even think we will find some hidden vein of strength when we are faced with death—some legendary toughness that will allow us to remain composed, even if we do not feel composed. Well, Ethan did not find that strength. When he'd first come to Florida and had gone out to ride his bike, he'd tried to battle his way through the heat by pretending he was as tough as Lance Armstrong. But when it came to cancer, Ethan was the famed cyclist's shadow. He was the antonym of Lance.

2

Winter in Clearwater was like summer in Detroit; the terms didn't always mean much. Detroit was a city with vapor constantly hovering threateningly in the sky, falling in gray or white drops and sometimes descending en masse, like someone had snipped the strings that held the clouds up high. Clearwater, on the other hand, could have been the capital of the Sunshine State. The notes Ethan had taken on the pier with his iPad, as he sought to capture the atmosphere of the sea and sky and gliding pelicans, also indicated it had been clear and sixty degrees. The next day was a little chilly, with temperatures in the low fifties, windy but still sunny—perhaps the absolute depth of Florida winter.

Ethan Clarke had realized early in his cancer journey that he no longer possessed the disposition of a Michigander. The shivering would begin almost exactly when the temperature dropped below sixty, and so, on a bleak midwinter day, he decided to stay inside and put on the heat. He had a warm dog curled up at his feet, and his best friend Sophie was visiting and cooking something that smelled delicious even while the meal was in its infancy. It could have been the perfect January afternoon, except that, as too often happened on these meds, Ethan felt sick. It was a head-swimming queasiness that gently pulsated from head to toe—no pain, just will-sapping sickness. The effects of chemotherapy on him were unpredictable. Sophie's food smelled good and he would eat a little, but still, the nausea was real. So he napped, stroked his dog, and talked with his friend, trying to keep thoughts of disease in the distance, out of sight, even if the feeling of disease was upon him.

He was conjuring images in his mind as he reclined in a soft chair, images that might help to stave off negativity. He pictured the many things that he was lucky to have and for which he was grateful. He tried to think of those things as often as possible.

Ethan was extremely fortunate to live in a part of the world that often caused his breath to catch and his eyes to widen: Clearwater, Florida, a town that dipped its toes in the Gulf of Mexico on one side and Tampa Bay on the other. Those images never failed to bring a smile to his lips. Clearwater was surrounded by beaches layered with gold and seas that were blue, deep, and full of fins and flashing tails.

Ethan was lucky he had a chocolate Labrador that, like most Labs, was a friendly, energetic animal, all smiles and wags and inquiring ears. Ethan often took him for walks early in the morning to the dog park on the beach, where he watched him bounce in and out of the waves, barking and panting with joy. He had a dog that was a companion, friend, and entertainer all rolled in soft fur.

Aside from the spectacular views, Ethan also realized how blessed he was to live by the ocean. Every time he visited the sea, he took a deep breath of salt-soaked air and made sure to thank God for his life. Aroused sea-senses truly were a gift from above: mouth-watering, nostril-flaring, eye-opening. The ocean was a treasure and Ethan marveled at it often.

Then there was work. When he pulled into the parking lot each day, unlike other folks he knew, the emotion he felt was not dread. He did not hate his profession and it did not cause him stress. He was lucky he had a good job for a strong company, and he was paid well for it. Sometimes it was boring, but the compensation allowed him to slice through the tedium until he reached the weekend.

Perhaps above all else, he was lucky to have his friend, Sophie, whom he had known since his time in Detroit. He would do anything for Sophie, and he'd recently discovered she seemed to feel the same way.

Rhythmically and with regularity, nausea would pull Ethan back to negativity. Then, sitting up, head between his knees, he would think about things that he had wanted since he was a child—physical things, because cancer and lifestyle had made him weak. He would search for talents and missing skills and imagine he had them, had had them since childhood. Ever since he'd first visited the Big House, University of Michigan Stadium, he had wanted to be good at football; since the Detroit glory days of the '80s, he had wanted to be good at basketball; and he had always wanted a better bike and the skill, time, and willpower to ride it faster.

Sophie was a sports fan, a supporter of all things Michigan. Through the fall, winter, and spring she followed the Tigers, Red Wings, and Lions, even though Ethan often tried to convince her to discover some home field allegiance, now that her home field was Tampa. Sophie was the epitome of a good part-time athlete, with smooth muscles and a big heart, which was one reason she'd moved from Michigan to Florida. She loved the outdoor life. It was rare to find this woman inside—she even drove a convertible.

Ethan was not an athlete—not an excellent athlete, anyway—but that was what he had always wanted to be. He was fine at football, could see and understand the game, and so committed to it physically. But a child stood out in youth football with arm strength, speed, or size, and he was small and slow. He could throw, but the ball left his hand without zip.

He was decent at basketball and again, could sense the game and appreciate it tactically. But as other boys embraced puberty and his body ambled through formative teenage years, he was left behind on the bench or in the stands with no outlet for his adrenaline or passion.

Being a victim of cancer and a victim of age was a depressing combination, but Ethan wondered: would it be more depressing for an athlete than a wannabe athlete? Was it better to have loved and lost, than never to have loved at all? It was never too late to improve, and Florida was awash with adult sporting options, but he could not see himself playing team sports, because he was sick and because he had not been good. Why struggle for mediocrity?

Visualization and imagery were important, and when it came to manipulating a ball through the air or through a hoop, he saw nothing. But maybe he could get back on his bike; surely he could get back on his bike, where prowess and success lived in the heart and mind, not in the eyes of a disappointed coach or teammate. It would depend on what happened in the next few weeks, how his psyche held up, but Ethan could see himself on a bike.

He had learned in the past few months that cancer did not just affect the physical. It affected the mental and metaphysical as well; cancer affected a man's soul, a man's heart, and a man's freedom. Cancer had sapped his physical strength; he found that out as soon as he tried to get out of bed after the operation and stumbled, grasping at a nurse for support. But it had also drained away all of his mental strength; he found that out the moment he received the news of the disease, when he felt his will seep down to his toes and then out, pooling at his feet like blood on a cold, disinfected tile floor.

Had it drained away his spiritual strength, too—that inner drive which had once found voice in youthful longhand writing and then in insightful journalistic typing? This was one reason for Ethan's decision to write once more. With Fat-Fingered Tony's smile in mind, he had begun quickly grasping at words like he had grasped at the nurse for support and guidance.

And in the meantime, while he looked for a way forward, there was courage to be found in two companions. What little Ethan had left to give he would give to a chocolate Labrador and a longtime friend. There were hidden qualities in a Labrador retriever, mysterious sensitivities, magical perceptions that meant he knew something was wrong whenever it was wrong and sought to help with a head on the knee or a lick on the face. And then there was Sophie, who gave out sustenance in loyal companionship. She just needed to hold Ethan's hand, look into his eyes and smile, and he felt calmer, stronger.

3

Sophie felt ambivalent as she finished the first few pages of Ethan's autobiographical exposé of survivorship. He had told her he was keeping track of his cancer journey in words and she had asked if she could read it.

"I would be honored, my friend," he had said with a wry smile. "No feedback, though. Enjoy, but enjoy quietly."

Ethan had always been happy to share his stories, poems, and essays. He enjoyed words, enjoyed the art of arranging words, and she enjoyed trying to understand her friend through his musings. This free flow of words, though, had started off in an uncharacteristically depressing manner. That was understandable, of course. Ethan had cancer. Why would he not be drowning in negative emotions, having been recently diagnosed?

From experience, Sophie knew that when you had met one cancer survivor, you had met *one* cancer survivor. The feelings, emotions, and reactions that one individual had would be different, whether to a small or very large degree, from those experienced by another individual. She felt ambivalence toward the journal because she was reading about a dear friend in trouble and that was hard. But she was also fascinated, as a woman who worked closely with cancer survivors, to see how Ethan would deal with his disease. She was in an ideal position to observe and assist as a friend, but now also to look inside his heart and mind as he wrote about his feelings, thoughts, and experiences.

His decision to write, she thought, was a healthy one. It gave him a very meaningful emotional outlet. Sophie had told her friend time and time again that his working life should revolve around words and not numbers, because words produced a smile while numbers caused a frown. But the use of the written word in this journal, so far, did not mirror the man himself, from Sophie's point of view. Though of course, point of view was all that mattered.

She saw her friend as sometimes quiet but always kind and funny. His interactions with people revealed a subtle charm that was gently enticing, and when he was focused on a passion, Ethan was eloquent and engaging.

He had talked often about his days as a *Free Press* reporter and described blending a love of words with a love for the city of Detroit. When he reminisced, thought back on that period in his life, it was with pleasure. He had also talked about his family, warts and all, but the portrayal combined love, compassion, and compassionate anger. His father had been a brute, but Ethan's fury was hot, not cold as it was in the pages she now read.

"Sophie, my family was as Detroit as Eminem driving a Ford Mustang. They were all down-to-earth, hardworking, passionate sports fans who lived in the city, shopped in the city and sometimes had a little too much fun in the city. My dad especially was a drunk, but a working-class drunk with character."

Now, on paper, these memories seemed overcast, overshadowed by disease. They did not reflect the Ethan Clarke she knew. When she thought of her friend and sports, she thought of a fighter, not a failure. She had heard tales of a scrappy athlete who competed in spite of physical limitations, and of a cyclist with the heart of Lance Armstrong if not the lungs.

Sophie had observed the many faces of cancer survivorship in her years working to care for those affected by the disease. She had seen both joy and despair in the face of death, and many emotions in between. One survivor, a Hispanic senior named Lena whom she had grown to love deeply, had laughed, danced, and sung her way through breast cancer, despite the pain of age, harsh radiation treatment, and even cultural and social stigma in her community. She had broken a hip line dancing, seventy-five years old and disease ridden but still pushing herself to have fun.

That was how Sophie thought she would act if she were ever diagnosed. But how you think you will act and how you will act—well, she hoped she would never have to find out. But her friend had discovered his own mortality, and at the moment, it seemed too heavy a burden to bear.

After Sophie finished reading the first few entries in her friend's journal, she was more than thoughtful. The sadness concerned her, but writing could have great cathartic possibilities, especially for Ethan, so there was hope, always hope. And she would be there for him, of course—they would travel this road together.

4

On his first visit to the Palm Harbor YMCA, Ethan Clarke sat in the lobby for a long time—too long—feeling sorry for himself, isolating himself. It was cool inside, in all senses of the word. The lobby was a haven from the oppressive Florida heat, and also a haven from the anxiety that, for many, accompanied exercise. It invited ease, with couches and coffee tables and smiles from staff of all shapes and sizes. The YMCA lobby was a place to inquire about exercise options, and relax after exercise, but it was also a place to talk and laugh and embrace aspects of wellness that did not involve movement or sweat. On several occasions Sophie had described the personality and functionality of a good YMCA lobby to her friend, and now he could see it for himself.

Ethan, however, should have been sweating, exercising in the fitness room with a group of fellow cancer survivors, not reflecting on the merits of an entrance way. He had his head down, earplugs in, listening to a new Coldplay CD and focusing on his iPad, the floor, the ceiling—anything but his fellow human beings.

Sophie worked for the YMCA, and had for about twenty years, but the organization had been relatively unknown to Ethan when she first met him. The only YMCAs he had seen were the Detroit and Ann Arbor Ys, which he knew only as a non-member. To him, the buildings were old, tall structures that housed the homeless, nothing more.

Ethan had become an accountant when he left school and often had reason to work in the downtown areas of both these cities. On many occasions, he'd driven by the Detroit Y, a towering, red-brick building that proudly called attention to itself and attention to a neighborhood that was old turn-of-the-century Detroit. In Ann Arbor, the structure was less imposing and fought for recognition in the midst of University of Michigan history and ambition.

One picture that did linger with Ethan, however, along with the bricks and mortar, was an image of purpose in the organization—purpose in the form of people served. In Detroit, residents, mostly African-American, came and went swiftly, or else lingered, pacing on sidewalks, leaning on walls, looking or waiting. Exercisers, Lycra-clad or hidden in bulky sweats, came and went also, but they were inconspicuous, almost secondary.

And in Ann Arbor, he saw a faded cream brick, turquoise-trimmed building, not as tall or ornate as the Detroit Y, but nonetheless a functional product of its time. It stood across from the library and provided both an outdoor social space and an indoor safe place to the same lost inhabitants— more racially mixed, perhaps, but all leaning, thinking, looking for life.

Ethan's view of the YMCA was just a view, with no investigation involved. He had some history, a theme tune in the back of his mind, a dance involving cowboys and Indians, but the Y was not relevant to his life and so was of no interest. He just saw a shelter for those that needed shelter, and then he returned his focus to the task at hand. And then, one evening in Nemo's bar and grill before a Detroit Red Wings game, a few of the cogs and wheels that dictate human existence clicked around, and Ethan's life changed. There was a fork in the path; the left turn looked more enticing, and his life was different after that night.

Nemo's was a Detroit institution, a roll-up-your-shirtsleeves, hard hat bar and grill that attracted working-class assembly-line patrons and suits all at the same time. Its reasons for being were comfort food, beer, and Motor City sports. People went for ten minutes or an hour before a home Red Wing hockey or Tigers baseball game, and then bundled up with other diehard natives in a Nemo's shuttle bus to travel to one of two old downtown arenas. Other fans went for the duration of a game, to eat and drink and watch any of the local teams: the Lions, Tigers, Pistons, or Red

Wings. It was a smoky, whaddya bar, full of opinions, retorts, screams, curses, and mostly hard-luck post-game stories.

It was in Nemo's that Ethan met this fascinating, funny lady. He made the decision to talk to a stranger in a bar, something he never did, because she was beautiful and animated in her conversation, and because as she realized Ethan was listening to her, she began to bad-mouth his alma mater, the University of Detroit, with a wink and a nod at his T-shirt and a tug at her own U of M baseball hat. Ethan never really understood how he managed to approach Sophie in her group, why he took a deep breath and walked up to converse in a manner that was clearly appealing to her. It had felt like a key moment at the time, like he had been picked up and moved to that spot for a reason, as part of a strategy.

"I'm not used to seeing Wolverines in the big city. Watching hockey and drinking beer, too? Is the Ann Arbor library closed?" He thought his opening line wasn't too bad.

"We come here occasionally, but there's never anyone to talk to. You Titans are normally too drunk to talk. Drowning your sorrows from all the sports beatings we put on you." Sophie's ripostes were smiling ripostes: playful.

"Our debate teams are good. Those contests were always pretty close. You guys were really good at discussions on Greek mythology and quantum physics, but we kicked your butts on American history and the birth of the auto industry."

The trash talk turned to small talk, and Ethan joined his new friend and her companions on the shuttle bus from Nemo's to the Joe Louis Arena so they could continue to get to know each other. That was when Sophie had first mentioned she worked at the Y. Ethan's first thought was, *In which part of those forbidding buildings could she possibly work?* Then, between periods, as they got beer and hotdogs in the crowded corridors that surrounded the rink, and as pockets of people talked about pad saves, slapshots, and fights, Sophie provided some background on her decision to move away from her original career, banking, and into fitness.

"The YMCA has such great depth and breadth, Ethan. It's an organization with a history of caring for many population groups; young factory workers far from home, war veterans, the homeless. But in recent years we've become more and more focused on health and wellness. It was such a simple thing for me in the end, realizing that I enjoyed a volunteer pastime, group exercise instructing, more than I did my full-time job in corporate banking relations. Honestly, the Y is now my life."

Ethan remembered multitasking at this first meeting. He remembered listening and answering Sophie, but in the back of his mind there were quick-fire questions flashing, like shooting stars. What creates a connection with a person? Is it instinctual—a smell, a taste, a sound, an ephemeral sensory strand that weaves between individuals and gently, quietly pulls them closer together? What is it about the sight of a smile that flows from eyes to mouth, the sound of a voice that teases, tells, and asks with interest? What is it about the words a person speaks? What makes those words resonate, hum, so that later, a phrase or sentence is still vibrating, repeating itself as sleep prevails? Love, of course—but also fate? What are the by-products when fate works its magic so well?

It was about ten years after he graduated that Ethan had moved down to Florida to work for Raymond James, a financial services company in Tampa. He had actually been enticed away by a head hunter, which was always fun, and when he flew down for the interview he'd fallen in love with the location just by flying over it, circling to land at the airport and seeing blue seas and white beaches, Tampa Bay and the Gulf of Mexico. The interview passed by with ease because it was like a factual face-to-face, with little probing outside defined lines. Ethan knew what he was good at and felt comfortable talking numbers, statistics, spreadsheets, and data-driven decision making. There had been no interest in anything outside of business on either side of the desk, which made the interaction simple for all.

It was not even a year after he moved that Sophie had come to Clearwater—another reason Ethan believed in fate and ties that bind. Sophie thought it was luck, although she did admit that her friend's regular calls, e-mails, handwritten letters, and all the descriptions Ethan gave her of Floridian life were an influence. She was also adamant that it was her career and the job at the YMCA of the Suncoast that had brought her south, not an unbreakable friendship or an outside guiding hand. There was also a messy divorce involved, but that erupted later and the postmortem, involving regretful tears, reflective wine, anger, and sadness, revealed a long-term relationship fissure that indicated relocation had been the straw that broke the camel's back, not part of the load that made the camel cry.

In Palm Harbor, Sophie became an executive director and also oversaw a program for cancer survivors called LIVE**STRONG** at the YMCA. This gave her some hope in the midst of the despair that followed Ethan's diagnosis. She was already working with cancer survivors, had seen many lives improved because of exercise during and after treatment, and was an exercise specialist herself—and so she felt that in many ways beyond just being supportive, she could help her friend, perhaps even help to heal him.

Ethan alone had been a weak, uninspired cancer survivor, lacking hope in so many ways. After Sophie convinced him to take her advice, he had come to the YMCA and spent most of his time hiding in the lobby while a new LIVE**STRONG** at the YMCA group received an orientation. He had decided he would rather retreat behind a mental barricade than socialize or learn or move in any way. Sophie tried not to be disappointed, to be as understanding as she was with all of the participants in her program. But it was hard, maybe because she expected more, or just wanted more from her friend. Maybe she was disappointed in Ethan's lack of fight, or perhaps his lack of respect for a disease that was too often triumphant. She felt cancer deserved or demanded to have more courage shown by its protagonists, if the battle were to be in any way fair.

Ethan felt bad, wished things could be different and, as a way of trying to appreciate his friend's efforts to help all survivors, found and read a welcome letter that Sophie had provided earlier.

Dear Friend.

*Welcome to LIVE**STRONG** at the YMCA: A Cancer Survivor Exercise Program. We are happy you are joining us and look forward to getting to know you.*

We have a few activities planned on the first day which will help you get acquainted with the YMCA's facility and other program participants. We will be taking a quick tour of the facility, so please wear comfortable shoes. You don't need to bring anything with you, but if you'd like, you may bring a family member, caregiver or friend.

On the first day, we will get to know each other, and I will explain more about the program. You will also fill out all the necessary forms and receive LIVESTRONG Foundation resources you will find valuable.

LIVESTRONG at the YMCA is a structured exercise program in a supportive environment. It is designed to improve your cardiovascular fitness, strength, balance, and flexibility. Regular attendance and participation creates the group experience in a supportive environment, which you'll discover is a valuable part of the program.

We understand that you may have appointments or commitments that cannot be changed. We just ask that you keep us informed if you are unable to make it to one of the sessions.

If you have any other questions about the program, please contact me. I look forward to seeing you soon!

Sincerely,
Sophie

It was a good letter, a welcoming letter, the kind of letter that might put a person at ease. That was one of the key aims of the LIVESTRONG at the YMCA initiative. Sophie had taken time to explain some of the details behind the program from her perspective during Ethan's first trip to the Y as a cancer survivor, when she had given him the letter. It was a more in-depth explanation than she might have provided to a regular participant, but Ethan thought she wanted him to embrace LIVESTRONG at the YMCA rather than just do it.

"Ethan, for the Y this is not just an exercise program, though exercise is of course important; it's about understanding the gaps that exist between how the YMCA and its staff are perceived by cancer survivors like you, and how we want to be perceived. It's about what the building looks like, how intimidating the environment is, and how welcoming the Y wants it to be."

Sophie had spoken with a businesslike conviction that her friend had not experienced before. She truly believed in what she did and felt very strongly that she and her organization could make a real difference in the community if given a chance.

"To be as effective as we can be, we need to improve how the Y as an organization is perceived by partners, the medical field in general, and cancer services in particular." Sophie furrowed her brow and looked intensely at her friend as she continued.

"For us, it's about how engaged and knowledgeable referring agencies are when it comes to the LIVE**STRONG** at the YMCA program and how likely they are to send a cancer survivor to the Y so that they can take part in exercise activities. Because if the survivors don't come, if they are not referred or don't hear about the program in some way, if they turn away at the door because they're scared, then it doesn't matter about the exercise program and how beneficial exercise is to a survivor."

Ethan felt good basking in Sophie's passion, but really he should have been an easy sell. He was her best friend, knew by heart the benefits that came with exercise, didn't need to be referred, didn't need to see a flyer or an ad; he was there and he was sold. But there was a gap that had opened up in his own mind, one not listed in the YMCA literature, a subconscious gap filled with trepidation. It was a chemical reaction between cancer and historical mental and emotional hang-ups that was making him freeze, like a deer in headlights.

5

Ethan was trying to think of ways to decipher his mood, to explain it, to help himself and to help Sophie understand. The self-examination came in written form, pages and pages of pondering, and in quiet contemplation with no company save the dog at his feet. He thought his friend felt disappointed because the help she could give, the help that happened to be her life's work, was not working, or was not emotionally suitable at that time. Ethan's mind was like a windy night in the city he loved: refuse whirling, gray shapes looming, dark alleys at every corner. He found it hard to distinguish the path ahead.

He thought Sophie also felt bad because she had broken a golden rule: she should not have been presuming to know what help her friend needed. Ethan could hear her again, patiently explaining a concept that was key to her work with cancer survivors:

"LIVE**STRONG** at the YMCA is about listening, caring, and guiding. It's not about knowing and telling. I do not know what a cancer survivor is going through because I have not had cancer. And even if I had experienced cancer—that would be *my* experience. Who am I to impose my experience on others?"

Ethan imagined his friend had abandoned, or sidestepped, those key principles with him because of their relationship. But to muddy the waters, and in her defense, how could she be expected to understand what he was feeling if he did not understand himself? Ethan thought if he could frame his emotions, give voice to them in his own head or on paper, perhaps he could explain better. The decision to write had been a good idea because thoughts flowed from a keyboard more freely, it seemed, than they did from his mouth.

The best interpretation he had was this: he felt like he was long-distance running and he was losing. No, he felt like he was long-distance running and had already lost—a feeling that was also a childhood memory.

Ethan had been a typical American boy, and certainly a typical Detroit boy. He saw success in sports. The activities he had always really wanted to be good at, desperately wanted to be good at, were football, basketball, and biking. Love of football was a regional expectation, the fate of any Detroit boy, or Michigan boy for that matter. He watched the sport religiously on TV, enjoyed the brutal athleticism on display and, beyond the physical, enjoyed the finesse that shone through in the shape of the quarterback's arm in motion before limb and man were crushed under the weight of linebacker force and flesh. Ethan was not an aggressive child, but he admired aggressiveness and the ability to thwart aggressiveness.

He had played football for a time in a local rookie league, but he'd been mediocre, made up the numbers as a body used alongside other bodies to frustrate those with talent. He played basketball in the same city leagues, in damp and dark school gymnasiums, with a similar lack of impact and, therefore, self-fulfillment.

Ethan had spent many childish hours pondering the reasons he was not good, was not even just a little better, at pastimes he loved. When he was young, he had been convinced he just suffered from physical disadvantages; as he grew a little older, he began to look around and see that he lacked raw talent; and as he got older still, he learned about and recognized a fear of failure.

As an adult, he decided that he probably would never have excelled in either sport, but also decided that he could have been much better if he had been told, or been coached, or just understood the fundamentals of sports psychology. In many instances, success for the less physically gifted involved possession of a risk-taker's mindset. Ethan was conservative on the field of play, usually overthought things, could never "just do it," and worried about losing more than winning. He could have overcome a lack of physical attributes if he had been mentally stronger.

He did have a bike while growing up, and on occasion raced his two wheels around Wyandotte, down Eureka Road or Biddle Avenue next to the river. It was hard to fly along in such an urban setting, but sometimes he would increase the risk and close his eyes briefly before opening them in fright. It was worth a scare for Ethan to see himself on an open road, on a sleek racing bike, gliding through forests, up winding hillsides, down smooth, car-less streets. He was in a peloton, for the blink of an eye, and it felt good.

His father was an amateur triathlete, and he had a state-of-the-art machine. On many occasions—sometimes reluctantly, sometimes excitedly, depending on the state of their relationship—Ethan had watched him race. He remembered going to see him one year when the swim portion of the race had occurred in the Detroit River. Then, Ethan's father had impressed his son by running and diving into the cold, dark water. But the best part of the race, as always, had been seeing the riders fly by on their bikes, arms tucked and heads down, dozens of aerodynamic blurs.

Ethan's parents finally divorced when he was in his early teens, which he felt exacerbated the experience. He'd been a turbulent teen, with his share of anger and righteousness, but, like many adolescents, he expected to be misunderstood by and rail at two parents who could provide a solid home, a ship from which he could peer out at and question the stormy, unjust seas of life. Ethan's parents separating, regardless of their troubles, was inconsiderate and, on a basic level, incomprehensible.

Among the many things he blamed his dad and the divorce for, never getting a good bike ranked high. His mom was not into biking, even less so when her husband left. She stayed in shape, liked to go to exercise classes with friends, enjoyed swimming, but especially liked to run. So, as a single, responsible parent conscious of the physical health and wellbeing of her child, she encouraged, even demanded, that her son run. His high school in Detroit had a tradition of athletic excellence and a relatively new, modern cinder running track in the football stadium, and so Ethan ended up on a track team with parental expectations.

But, with a stomach-churning passion, he loathed running. He would wake up long before a practice or meet just to lie there, dreading the wake-up knock at the door, or would sit in math or physics class and actually hope for the lesson to drag on so he didn't have to run after school. Even at a tender age, Ethan realized his issues were as much psychological as physical, as much about mind games and motivation as they were about talent. He was never the best runner on the squad, nor the worst. He would most likely have improved had he been able to banish his barriers, the same old barriers: lack of focus, lack of confidence, and fear of losing. Sports psychology then was a laughable topic, especially to high school coaches who lived by statistics and dreamed of sending players to the Big Ten Conference.

But a bigger psychological problem with running, more damaging than other issues, was that Ethan was bored by running, and running allowed his mind to wander, often back to home life. He enjoyed the variety, the action, and the many different elements that made up a football or basketball game, even when he was not playing the game well. But when he ran, around and around and around the track, it felt like he was being punished—even more, tortured. There were times when he wanted to be successful at track because it was important to his mom. But those times were rare.

Thinking back, Ethan realized that there had of course been more emotions in play, because his dislike of track had been interwoven with the complex feelings that followed his parents' divorce. When his dad won a race (and he was good), the actual victory came at the end of the run, after the swim and bike. So Ethan would see him running across the finish line with a triumphant grin on his face. The grin and the triumph tore him in half and that was what he thought about when given the time, running around and around that cinder track.

It had been three months since Ethan had been diagnosed with cancer, and even before the diagnosis, he had felt like he was walking in sand every day. He was lethargic, achy, and breathless; he had a full, bloated feeling, and the minutes and hours of any given day would drag on. Like many survivors, particularly male survivors, it had taken him too long to admit that something was wrong and then too long to see a doctor. Consequently, life was drudgery; and what finally caused him to seek help was the recognition that not only was he unwell, but the sense of despair he was feeling resembled a particular period of his childhood.

When the doctor told Ethan he had cancer, he had actually used a couple of sports clichés to try to encourage him, without realizing that "you are in a race for your life" might depress his patient further, not persuade him to run faster. Ethan's cancer experience allowed him to understand that the endlessness of a race, the solitude of a race, that time in his life coincided with the aftermath of his parent's break-up. The more he thought and remembered, the more credence he gave to the tragedy of that youthful time, and the more he struggled to see a way past the disease, a way that did not end in despair.

That kind of analogy, though, Ethan knew, would be a tough sell with Sophie. His friend was a very practical person. She recognized that exercise was a means to an end and so she reveled in the experience. She understood that running, biking or competing led to results and she wanted those physical, spiritual, and mental results; she wanted to be fit, healthy, and well.

She also got exasperated by the kind of involvement Ethan had in sports. She was a fan, but could watch a game and be excited by a win and a little dejected by a loss, and then she could move on. Her friend, on the other hand, was plunged into despair at the very thought of his team losing and catapulted to the heights of ecstasy by the idea that they might win.

Tom Brady was a wonderful example of the unhealthy fanaticism that could eat away at Ethan Clarke. Ethan should have been a Detroit Lions fan, but Tom Brady had been the quarterback at the University of Michigan and Ethan had seen him play a few times, watched him inside a cauldron of blue and maize fervor; and since Brady was drafted by New England, New England was Ethan's team. Watching Michigan and Brady in person, in a stadium they called the Big House, involved becoming absorbed in the spectacle and emotion of a contest in a way that could not happen on the couch in front of a television. The experience enthralled him; and of course no one had more influence on a gridiron contest than the quarterback, and so that figure, distant on the field of play, was loved. Eventually, under intense cross-examination from Sophie, Ethan was honest with himself and was able to admit that he was not really a New England fan, he was a Tom Brady fan.

There was something about excellence that consumed Ethan—and when, after three Super Bowl victories, Brady had a perfect season in 2007, winning all his regular and post-season games before the final victory was ripped out of his grasp in the final minutes of the final game, Ethan was inconsolable for over a week. Sophie would ask why; she would tell her friend it was just a sport and explain that Brady had three rings on his finger, countless millions in the bank, and a supermodel wife on his arm.

"What is there to be sad about, really?" she would ask.

Ethan couldn't explain it, other than the losing, and maybe the nearly winning, and, more exactly, the thought of all those particular moments and plays when the losing and the nearly winning merged together to form defeat. It was the "what ifs" that really got him. And that was an overarching question he had about his cancer. What if?

6

~

Sophie had fond memories of Nemo's and her first meeting with Ethan, too. Of all the sports that she liked—and she liked all sports—hockey was her favorite. The ritual of going to Nemo's to eat, drink, and indulge in pre-game banter with fellow Red Wings fans was almost as enjoyable as the game itself. Now she knew it had been foreshadowing when her husband Jeff revealed that he did not like hockey. It was a doomed marriage from that moment, because what guy doesn't like hockey, and why wouldn't he have told his girlfriend that on one of the many Red Wings date nights they'd had?

In many ways, for her, Detroit had been a hard city to live in. Her family had relocated from Texas when she was a teenager, and just moving at that time in her life had been tough. They did not live in the city limits, but in a very affluent suburb called Grosse Point—but suburb and city alike felt the brisk winds that came off of Lake Michigan, Erie, and Huron in the winter, icy blasts all around. It was the winters that she found truly tough, and the many "hardships" that came as by-products of that long, bleak season.

But there were upsides to the area, and the main ones were Detroit sports and the YMCA. Ethan was right: she did not become engulfed in sporting contests in the same way he did. She enjoyed the festivities that surrounded each event as much as the game itself, and in fact hardly watched sports on television, preferring to be at live games. It was the food, drink, conversation, and rival trash talk before a game—and the hubbub, singing, cursing, and more trash talk during the game—that she really liked. The contest itself was always absorbing, and she was a great admirer of athletic prowess—but the outcome, the score, the effect on leagues, divisions, trophies—none of that mattered. Well, perhaps it mattered, but a loss did not ruin her evening, let alone several days of her life.

When she first saw Ethan, Sophie had thought he was a stud in a Titan's T-shirt, ripe for razzing. He was a skinny stud, but great looking with a thoughtful face that stood out in Nemo's, where thinking was optional but drinking necessary. It took four or five standard jibes, back and forth, before she became intrigued. Here was a man who was a little nervous, who was not trying to pick her up, but wanted to get to know her and genuinely wanted to listen.

That was a trait that Ethan Clarke did not give himself enough credit for—his willingness to listen and to try to understand. It was very rare, in men especially and certainly in a man in a Detroit bar; and during that very first meeting, a very meaningful connection had been made. As their relationship grew, she had come to admire many other qualities in her friend, qualities that only strengthened that connection.

Sophie could not imagine coming from a broken home. While she had experienced her share of teenage angst, she also recognized early in life that she was privileged and loved. She had never wanted for anything, and had two parents who adored her and adored each other.

Ethan was not that lucky, but regardless, he had been rock solid for his family through good and bad times. His part-time job with the *Free Press* was a labor of love, but it also brought money into the household. The job in accounting that he tolerated but never really liked brought even more money into the household. Ethan had a brother and a sister, and he had helped put them through school and allowed them to fly the coop early while he stayed with and supported their mom. When his family as a whole was back on its feet emotionally and financially, he had finally mustered the strength to break away and move to Florida.

What Sophie admired about her friend was his doggedness and work ethic. He did not see himself as successful, but success came in many forms.

This was not a passive man who let things happen to him, though passivity had become a symptom of his disease. He had an inner strength that, at the moment, during the early stages of his cancer journey, was not being exercised.

Sophie's own move to Florida had been emotional because of the disintegration of her marriage, but in many ways it had been a liberating and fun experience. That there could have been so many positives during the divorce proceedings was entirely due to the friendship she had with Ethan. He allowed her to put aside anxiety so she could bask in the sunshine; he helped wipe tears from her cheeks and made sure the tears were replaced by sea and sand. She could not have had a better, more supportive friend. And now it was her turn.

Her turn, she thought, might take many forms. Certainly she planned to continue to encourage him to become a part of the LIVE**STRONG** at the YMCA program. She believed passionately in the benefits of exercise for cancer survivors, and alongside her own belief, she had statistics. Exercise could help prevent cancer, prevent its recurrence, and aid in recovery.

Sophie also planned to be a supportive friend—perhaps more supportive than she had been. She felt like she had been prescriptive and somewhat overbearing at first, while Ethan was trying to come to terms with his disease and the ways he wanted to handle it going forward. It was his journey, and she needed to respect the path he wished to walk, while listening and carefully offering guidance and support.

Except there was one nagging opinion she had about her friend, an opinion she had had for many years, but which now took on more urgency. Sophie thought Ethan should be more open—no, not more open, but *open*—about his homosexuality. She had known he was gay a few hours after they first met. There had been a level of conceit in her conclusion, but it had proved correct. When Ethan Clarke had not tried to pick her up that night, after the connection they had made, she knew he was gay.

They had talked, and he had eventually been open with her, but had asked that she keep the knowledge of his sexuality to herself. She had pushed back a few times, but without force—but now she wondered if she needed to push harder. She felt there were too many correlations between

Ethan's handling of his cancer diagnosis and Ethan's handling of his sexual orientation. Her personal opinion was that the benefits of being honest about both far outweighed the benefits of being secretive. Maybe more subconsciously than consciously, she felt that her friend worried about the stigma that surrounded being gay and having cancer. He had been successful at hiding his sexuality, and now he was struggling to be open about his cancer—when support systems lay all around.

But who was she to impose her opinions on anyone? Ethan was her friend for many reasons, but there was a quirkiness to him that she really loved. He was overtly masculine in many ways—his strength of will, loyalty, stubbornness, and addiction to sports—but he also had good feminine traits. Standout among those was his willingness to listen without needing to tell her what to do. One male characteristic she did not understand though, was his inability—or unwillingness—to reveal emotions or seek emotional support. His answer to her insistence that he open up about his sexuality was: whose business was it but his? So, again she thought, who was she to impose her opinions on anyone, especially a friend who was caring enough to not impose on her?

7

As a person who had never really embraced Christianity, Ethan felt hypocritical asking God for help. Nevertheless, he had done so a couple of times since his cancer diagnosis, and did so again as he looked out of his dining room window at the majestic live oak tree shading his yard. The tree had a trunk that was about six feet in diameter, a strong, muscular base that allowed thick long branches to curl and curve up and out, looking for Floridian sunshine. Along with the imposing nature of the tree, one of its unique features was the way it was dressed. Long strands of green and blue moss hung from every limb, providing delicate motion in a breeze to match sturdy swaying in a wind.

Ethan had come to know the tree well, because he had spent too many hours looking out of his window, watching the people on the avenue at work and play. He had pushed his dining room table out of the center of the room and against a wall so that he could sit with his laptop, type, and stare out at the activity. He now knew the times that Betty walked her golden retriever in the morning, a functional walk that allowed his neighbor, an overweight smoker, to get out of the house for her morning cigarette and Yankee, her fourteen-year-old dog, to totter over to the yard next door to do his business before going back to sleep. He knew what time Don loaded up his truck with ladders and tools so that he could leave to work on the new senior center in Tarpon Springs—and he particularly enjoyed watching two sets of kids, the Morgan twins and Lucy and Bailey Johnson, leave for school, all screams and laughs, bursting with an abundance of energy that only preteens possessed.

The only respite he had from this daily inertia involved two close confidants and companions. Very early in the morning, sometimes before five o'clock, he would roll out of bed, foggy and stiff, to be greeted by another example of abundant energy, this time released in wags and whines. It was a short drive over to a small neighborhood park where Ethan would sit on a bench and watch Jay explore. The dog would sniff and search for a while before bringing him a stick to throw. The ritual was repeated at teatime, when there were other dogs around to join in the fun.

Then there was Sophie—he thanked God for Sophie, with real sincerity and belief. She allowed him to pause, to breathe, to gather himself, to feed off the love and compassion that flowed from her whenever they were together, happy or sad, angry or contented. He told her often that she spent too much time with him, that as gregarious as she was, she needed to share her joy with other friends. But each time the subject was broached, she would just smile.

"Ethan, not only are you a friend in need, but you have cancer. I live for my friends, but I also work with and for cancer survivors. Tell me, why *wouldn't* I be spending so much time with you?"

Each time Sophie made such a statement, she would smile and squeeze Ethan's hand. That smile and her touch were like fresh air, and her commitment and compassion tore him apart, because he was finding it so hard to reciprocate. One simple thing he could do to bring happiness to his good friend would be to get up and visit her YMCA. Why was this a hard thing to do? Sophie had told him he needed psychological support along with physical support, and that such a need was common among cancer survivors because diagnosis was traumatic, as was the onset of the disease itself. And Ethan understood the strengths and weaknesses of the mind. The array of personal and professional sporting analogies he collected were testament to his belief in the mountains that could be moved, or pebbles left untouched, because of willpower or lack of willpower, respectively.

Then, one morning, he returned to the Y. An hour spent staring at a tree, acknowledging hundreds of years of consistency and strength, had finally brought him back. This time he made it into class, but his mental fortitude seemed to evaporate as soon as he was surrounded by fellow survivors. He sat in his chair like a victim of shock, looking down at his knees as classmates spoke words of feeling and emotion that could have been comforting, but instead filled the air like rain clouds, gathering around Ethan's head. He held onto his seat, fingers tight to the chair.

There were six individuals in the class, including Ethan: survivors who were different in so many ways, but united by cancer. They sat in a circle, introducing themselves and listing the goals they had set for this new LIVE**STRONG** at the YMCA session. The other five individuals had already met with either Sophie or her colleague Jenny one-on-one, so that they could describe their physical limitations, their likes and dislikes with regard to exercise, and any specific experiences they'd had while going through treatment.

Ethan knew that the one-on-one session was a detailed wellness interview and key to the safety and success of the program, but when Sophie had tried to make his appointment, his response was short and sharp, full of stubbornness coated in fear. He'd told her that she knew everything about him, so what was the point? And then he had turned away, ashamed.

Three of the participants in the class were women, with an equal number of men. This was unusual in Sophie's experience. She had speculated, while encouraging Ethan to participate, that men were often slower in admitting they had health issues and slower still in seeking help for those issues. That there were three male survivors in the group was wonderful news to her.

All of the survivors present seemed steady and strong in spite of the disease that ravaged them, but still, Ethan could not raise his head. He knew he was being discourteous, refusing to look these people in the eye when they were talking, but he could not help himself. The sadness and reality in the room was oppressive, heavy, and Ethan was a survivor who did not feel like he had survived or could survive anything. He did try to listen, realized he should listen, even with his head bowed. He knew he needed to attempt to understand, for himself and out of common decency, because they were reintroducing themselves and sharing their experiences for his benefit as a newcomer.

Ethan listened, and in spite of himself, heard character in each voice. Cancer seemed to be a subplot in lives full of richness. The disease had not engulfed this group as it was threatening to engulf him.

He heard Suzanne tell a story about her weekend attempts to find a bird feeder that was squirrelproof. Apparently she was an animal lover, and enjoyed bird watching, but ravenous squirrels were ruining her pastime. As something of an aside, she shared that she was still undergoing treatment for multiple myeloma.

Brenda told the group that she was a two-time survivor, two months out of treatment for this bout of breast cancer, and she was amazed at the variety of programs that the YMCA offered. Apparently she had not been an exerciser, and LIVE**STRONG** at the YMCA had brought her to the Y for the first time.

Steve, by contrast, had been a member at Palm Harbor since the branch had opened, and at the Clearwater Y before that. He was a fitness fanatic, an early-morning attendee at cycling classes, a triathlete, and—Ethan's ears pricked up—a former University of Florida wide receiver who had had trials with the Tampa Bay Buccaneers. Steve had esophageal cancer. He told the class that he had moped for a few days, disappointed that, with an active lifestyle and a careful diet, he had still succumbed to this disease—but then had plunged back into exercise, perhaps with even more zeal than before.

Dave was a little older and quieter than Steve, but told everyone that he was a prostate cancer survivor who was also caring for a son with liver cancer. Then, last but not least, Norma shared that she was just beginning treatment for breast cancer—and had the same squirrel problems as Suzanne!

Ethan spoke, but it was quick, mumbled, and forced, and when everyone stood to move into the exercise room, he took his opportunity to flee. He excused himself, taking his bag with him so he could sit in an armchair in the lobby, near the front doors. There was sunshine and air there, and a glimpse of blue sky that seemed to induce calmness. This meant Ethan could breathe and relax and add little notes, thoughts, and feelings in words or short sentences on his iPad. This simple act allowed for a further release of tension and, finally, there was relative normality.

The liberation that came with writing mirrored past times when conflict had been calmed by words conjured and typed. Maybe it was the single-mindedness of the act, the fact that Ethan could talk to himself, create for himself, without worrying about interaction or opinion—until he was ready for interaction and opinion. Maybe it was because he didn't have to rely on anyone or feel relied upon. Or maybe it was just the fact that he liked to write and felt good at it, when he didn't like or feel good about much else.

Sophie was upset again, though, in a caregiver kind of way. Someone must have told her that Ethan had left the session, so she came out of her office to check on her friend. He couldn't give much of an explanation, and found it hard to express himself, even though Sophie was using her active listening skills and probed with open-ended questions and non-judgmental comments. Ethan just didn't feel like exercising, didn't want to tell her why he didn't feel like exercising, and didn't want to analyze at what point he'd stopped feeling like exercising. He didn't want to be listened to. Eventually she understood and stopped, and he followed her back into her office to mope and watch her work.

Sophie had come to Ethan's house that day to pick him up, because he hadn't felt well enough to drive and he lived fairly close. Since he was finished earlier than either had expected and Sophie did not have time to leave, he sat quietly in a corner chair, typing. She had a conference call, and when she was finished, she would take him home. In the meantime, Ethan toyed with words on his screen, creating and erasing, playing with prose—and he listened, too.

His friend was actually very involved in LIVE**STRONG** at the YMCA on a national level. The whole program had originally been a test partnership between the LIVE**STRONG** Foundation and the YMCA of the USA, because data showed that it wasn't good to just rest during or after cancer as most doctors had once recommended—it was actually better to be active in some way. The LIVE**STRONG** Foundation wanted to see how they could make exercise available to as many individuals diagnosed with cancer as possible—and the Y, of course, was everywhere.

Sophie's YMCA had been one of the first test sites, along with nine others around the country, and the experiment was so successful and so well received that eventually it had expanded to over two hundred Ys. She had been deeply involved, passionate, and was so good at what she did that she was asked to help to continue the growth of the program, and also to form an alumni network that would allow staff members to stay connected after their YMCAs had graduated from the expansion process.

The conference call involved people in Boise, Syracuse, Dallas, Asheville, and Ethan's old stomping ground, Ann Arbor. Sophie had the call on speaker, and the topic was the agenda for an upcoming conference in Austin, a conference hosted by the LIVE**STRONG** Foundation itself. The individuals talking with Sophie sounded like a feisty, humorous bunch, analyzing details, laying out plans, and discussing serious issues while simultaneously poking fun at each other.

It was interesting that these people all worked with cancer survivors. They sounded jovial and relaxed as they went about their business, moved off on unrelated tangents, and then came back to business. Someone volunteered to present an opening thought at the conference, and then they discussed the keynote speaker, Anna Schwartz, a noted cyclist and survivor who was also an expert in the field of exercise and cancer.

The LIVE**STRONG** Assembly, as it was called, was going to be a gathering of invited representatives from many organizations funded by the foundation. There were also going to be over sixty Y staff members in attendance, so Sophie and her colleagues were creating work groups and brainstorming activities around different topics so that the YMCA could take advantage of this get-together and use it as a learning and sharing opportunity.

This relaxed style of business continued, and it intrigued Ethan. Perhaps it was part and parcel of a job that was enjoyed, or was meaningful; or perhaps it appeared when there was such a level of respect held for colleagues involved in the work. Whatever the reason for the relaxed atmosphere, he listened to the rhythm of the chatter and laughter, let the flow of charitable industry and friendship wash over him, until he felt like he was going to fall asleep. Then he put his head down and let the listening go and the tiredness come.

Ethan felt ashamed at the way he had acted earlier that day. The level of his post-diagnosis selfishness was embarrassing, and he did not feel that cancer was an excuse. His aloofness in class, then his rudeness, falling asleep in Sophie's office—all of his actions that day had been depressing. Still, his friend acted like a friend, and Sophie drove him home as he dozed fitfully some more, the twists and turns of small town Palm Harbor causing his head to bounce against the side window. Fatigue was a constant side effect of Ethan's condition and the medication, and his friend understood that better than anyone. Perhaps that was why she was so forgiving.

Ethan tried to make up for his earlier tiredness by being industrious with his writing once he made it home. He was physically tired of being sick, and also mentally tired of thinking sick, so he turned to his source of solace. Writing—developing thoughts, typing thoughts—flushed his system for a while, expunging depression and replacing it with, if not happiness, then at least creativity.

During a break in typing, Ethan turned on the television and sipped at a cup of soup. *American Idol* was on, and the kaleidoscope of emotions on display eventually sucked him in and allowed him to relax for at least an hour. It was the auditions, and there were thousands and thousands of people lined up to get into a studio to sing in front of the judges. Many of the potential contestants were deliberately bizarre, many were unintentionally bad, and some were good; but all were having fun.

Well, that one wasn't; he was a bundle of nerves and the words from his song were stuck somewhere in his throat; and another one wasn't having fun because she had just been turned down and was bitter and angry. But generally, people saw an opportunity to dream, to turn away from routine and look for hope, and they plunged in enthusiastically.

Ethan did not watch much television, but *American Idol* had become an exception. It was an exuberant show, entertaining but competitive, and so it provided an easy release for him after work. He liked this group of judges: Steven, Jennifer, and Randy. They were knowledgeable, credible, caring, and articulate when they analyzed and criticized, but with enough of a tough streak to weed out individuals with egos bigger than their talent. And he liked Ryan Seacrest. Ethan could picture having a beer with Ryan. As he watched this particular show, he realized that the *Idol* host reminded him a little of Steve, the cancer survivor in his class, facially if not physically.

Ryan Seacrest seemed to have perfected a persona that was part next door and part Hollywood mansion. He mingled with moms and dads, little sisters, friends, and aunts, and chatted, joked, got to know them, commiserated, or celebrated. He provided the piece of *American Idol* that most contestants would remember long after the trauma of their audition faded: the warmth of their ten-minute relationship with Ryan.

After fifteen minutes or so of forgetful indulgence in the show, Ethan began to think again about his personal situation and the mental and physical roadblock he had encountered because of cancer and because of his own innate hang-ups. He began to truly recognize the depth of his fear of failure—and there were reminders of the perils of taking a chance in front of him, on the screen, one person after another exploding in tears, sobs, or profane outbursts—reminders of the perils of stepping out of the box.

Ethan turned off the television and sat once more at the window to look at his tree. He wanted to analyze his condition once more, to search for a way out of the maze, and so he looked up at gnarled branches and dangling moss. The full moon that shone through the tree reminded him of floodlights at an evening University of Michigan football game. There he was, fixating on sports again—but perhaps that was not a bad thing. Sophie wanted to help him using exercise—there was good evidence that exercise was helpful to survivors—but Ethan equated exercise with sports.

Ethan had hated losing in sports when he was younger, hated trying to compete in sports when deep down he was aware of his limitations. Recently he had begun to hate watching defeat in sports and, in fact, had acknowledged this flaw in a clear and decisive manner: if he thought his team was going to lose, he turned off the television.

Ethan understood the absurdity of what he was doing as he was doing it, knew it was more than defeat—more like cowardice, abdication of a responsibility to fight, to will, to hope, to support. He knew that what he was watching was only a game—and that competition was what games were about. Someone had to lose.

He thought often about his self-nominated position as the antonym of Lance. When the going got tough, Lance gritted not just his teeth but his whole body—and the bodies of those around him, his team. When the going got tough, he got going on his bike, in races, ignoring opponents, accidents, mountains, and most of all, pain. He forced himself to succeed, and that mentality clearly crossed over to his fight with cancer.

Ethan could not look at himself in the mirror, because he had cancer, could hardly sit in a room with a group of good, honest, determined people, because they also had cancer; and when he was around cancer, he smelled defeat. And that was really too bad, because he had the disease—and so defeat hung in the air, hung from his limbs like dead moss, making him a weak, sick version of the live oak in his yard.

8

The Big Tree in Rockport, Texas, was a live oak estimated to be over two thousand years old. Ethan had been doing some research during the night, while he looked out of the window, wide awake, wondering how old his tree was, how many sunrises it had seen and how many men and women had lived and died while claiming the tree as their own.

He had not been able to sleep. Defeatism had clung to him, like a layer of cold sweat, making him wrinkle his nose, weep a little, and think—too many thoughts. The sun and his dog's cold nose had brought a deep breath and a decision to try. A long night of introspection had finally led him to an understanding that this was actually not a game—that if he didn't find a way to come to terms with the fact that he had a life-threatening disease, he wouldn't just lose, he would lose his life.

All roads kept pointing back to the YMCA. It was the only outlet Ethan knew, his only tangible way of fighting back. The hardest thing was walking in the door, but that was also the best thing, because it allowed him to see Sophie's face light up. It made him understand that he was not only disappointing her with his attitude, but more importantly, he was scaring her. After they hugged, he walked away from her office, toward the wellness center to find Jenny, to see if she was available to listen and help.

Jenny was with a member and would be a few minutes, so Ethan sat, took a few deep breaths, and continued trying to build himself up. Aside from his psychological issues, there were many other reasons why he might feel a sense of trepidation as he sat contemplating exercise. Cancer, of course, and then the chemotherapy pills, a couple a day, which were adding to an overall sense of exhaustion.

Earlier in the morning, after he had finally left his seat by the window to try to shower himself out of his funk, Ethan had looked online for some facts on the particular medicine he was taking. Some of the facts he'd read were disturbing—even more so than the typical material on medications and their side effects. He found two particularly interesting articles about Mitotane on a website called Science Blog. Two lines stood out:

> Last week's *New England Journal of Medicine* marked a key study on an old drug, Mitotane, that is a structural derivative of the pesticide DDT and is used to treat adrenocortical carcinoma . . . Adrenocortical carcinoma is a rare cancer with only 16–38% of patients surviving for five years.

While much of the blog was incomprehensible, Ethan did find some alarming key words and phrases. The fact that Ethan's form of cancer had such a dire survival rate was cause for bleak thinking, and the fact that he was taking a derivative of DDT to try to combat the cancer did not make him feel any better. All he could recall about DDT were its devastating effects on the environment as a pesticide spray and its cancer-causing qualities. Now he was swallowing a pill containing it.

He had received some literature with the medication, and, as usual, he had not paid attention to it, but over breakfast he had spread the paperwork on the table. Again, key points stood out on the page.

> Tell your doctor if any of these symptoms are severe or do not go away: loss of appetite, nausea, vomiting, diarrhea, depression, lack of energy, unusual drowsiness, feeling that the room is spinning, changes in vision, rash, or changes in skin color.
>
> Some side effects can be serious. If you experience any of these symptoms, call your doctor immediately: abdominal or side pain, confusion, fast heartbeat, high fever or shaking chills, excessive sweating. Mitotane may cause brain or nervous system

damage when taken at high doses for longer than two years. Talk
to your doctor about the risks of taking this medication.

Layers of reinforcing facts were threatening to engulf Ethan. He finally
understood that not only did he have cancer—and a particularly ravenous
form of the disease—but he was also taking poison to try to kill the cancer.
These somber details had helped reinforce his decision to return to the
Y, this time with an increased level of conviction. He needed to try to do
something practical to survive.

Eventually Jenny was available to see him, even though he had just
turned up out of the blue. She was working with Ethan's group, the
survivors he should have connected and been exercising with by now, but
she had a colleague who could get them started so that the two of them
could take some time to talk.

Jenny seemed to have quite a sunny disposition, constant and level, no
matter the situation she found herself in or the individual with whom she
was working. Ethan felt better just sitting across from her, seeing her smile
and hearing her talk in such a reassuring way.

She began by explaining her style and the style of the YMCA when it
came to working with members.

"The Y philosophy in general involves starting slowly, gradually, not
doing anything excessive. This approach is even more important when cancer
is involved. When you begin to exercise as part of the LIVE**STRONG** at
the YMCA program, if you feel tired at any point, it's okay to sit, to rest,
or even to stop."

As Jenny talked, Ethan could see the similarity between her approach
and Sophie's. It was clearly a trained technique as well as a personality trait.
He felt calmer and more reassured the longer she talked.

"Tell me about your current exercise level, Ethan."

He chuckled. "It is pretty nonexistent at the moment, I hate to say.
I know it's important, but I'm a great example of the difference between
knowing and doing."

"Okay, so you aren't really exercising, but you understand the
importance of exercise. Is that what I hear you saying?"

He nodded.

"So what have you done in the past? When you think of exercising, what is it that makes you feel good?"

Ethan told a few of his running stories, but she seemed particularly interested in his past love of cycling.

"So it sounds like you really don't like running, but you enjoy cycling—so much so that you bought a brand new Schwinn—but the bike has mostly stayed dusty in your garage. Is that a fair summary?"

They spent a long time discussing his type of cancer, the operation he had had, how well the operation area was healing, and what treatments he was taking. Jenny was thorough, and that was before they had even begun to exercise. Her technique of constantly summarizing what she thought he had said was interesting because it forced Ethan to listen and to add or change the content if necessary. She wanted to know exactly what he was thinking, what he wanted out of her, and what he wanted out of the YMCA.

Having her then show him around the wellness center proved how thoroughly out of shape Ethan was. It was tiring to keep up, even when he wasn't doing anything—just following and listening and watching as she gave an overview of cardio machines he was interested in and the weight machines that might help him with his goals, demonstrating how they worked, slowly and carefully.

"Ethan, regaining strength and lost muscle is as important as working on the endurance levels you once had, but I need to reiterate that I want you to start really gently. When you're ready to advance, we can work on it together." Jenny gently grasped his elbow and looked him in the eye as she made this point.

"I'll help you figure out the next phase of your exercise program, what you want to work on, and how to increase your time on a bike or add to the weight you can lift safely. Even better," and Jenny gave him her biggest smile when she suggested this, "we could find a partner for you who is a survivor, so that you can help each other. For now, it's enough to understand that there are a lot of options available for you to do a lot of things if you want to, but just pedaling gently on a recumbent bike would be a wonderful place to start."

Ethan Clarke was a forty-five-year-old man, so he found it both humbling and soothing to have a young woman kneeling down to explain a console and the stop and start buttons on a basic bike trainer, encouraging him as he pushed the pedals at an excruciatingly slow pace. But to Jenny, that slow pace was a victory, and she squeezed his arm and pumped her fists in the air as he went slightly faster and then found a pace that was sustainable.

She was very good. Ethan had watched her a couple of times through the wellness floor windows when he had been hiding in the lobby, and he'd noticed that she clearly had different approaches for different people. She had listened to his sports tales and biking stories and judged him as a man who would like excitement, and she was right. It made Ethan feel good that she was encouraging him in such an enthusiastic way—made him feel like he was winning, not losing. For others, she was very low key, not drawing attention to them, quietly encouraging.

But he was showing off; when Jenny moved on to say hello to other members in the room, Ethan had to stop quickly as a wave of fatigue and nausea engulfed him. He had been on the recumbent bike for perhaps two minutes, and he had already overexerted himself. He had hastily set himself a goal to be on a real bike in a week, but it didn't look like that was going to happen.

Still, when he looked around, he realized that no one was laughing, and no one was staring. The other survivors were on their own bikes or treadmills, or were lifting weights in pairs. The world had not come to an end. So, he took a deep breath, thought back to his running days in Detroit, and began pedaling again at the same slow pace, two minutes at a time.

The comparison between running all those years ago and this new attempt to exercise had validity. It was all about focus and making it to the end, which was the reason Ethan didn't like to run. There was no joy in the act; it was all about making it through—making it through each lap and making it through each practice and making it through each meet. He had been running for other people and not for himself. Here, he was pedaling for his life, and again, there was no joy in that. Admittedly, he was averse to the task for purely selfish reasons; either he did it, or he would succumb to self-pity and cancer. But the fatigue that rolled in like waves meant it was an ordeal, minute by minute.

The YMCA was not a place for mirrors. Sophie had explained that, since the Y's primary focus was on health seekers who were often very self-conscious about body image, having mirrors everywhere was counterproductive. It did not encourage those who already felt discouraged. But Ethan didn't need a mirror to tell what he looked like on his bike.

Sophie had always made fun of the fact that he was skinny at six feet two and usually 165 pounds. Post-cancer, however, he looked gaunt. It was common to hear descriptions of cancer in military terms: a war, a fight, a battle. Well, he had begun to look like a prisoner of that war, undernourished and worn down. Cancer, and, more to the point, the treatment for cancer, had caused Ethan to lose even more weight—not a huge amount, but it was visible. He now weighed about 155 pounds, and it felt like most of that extra ten pounds had been lost from his leg muscles alone. They were crying out for the torture to end.

He cycled for about eight minutes, in two-minute increments. It would have been laughable, if Ethan had been able to laugh, but Jenny came back and encouraged him as he left the bike. She squeezed his shoulder and walked him to a chair at the back of the wellness center, where he could sit and recover while the rest of the group finished.

His fellow survivors around the room stood out because they were all wearing yellow shirts. Ethan remembered a few discussions about this, one involving Sophie on the phone with her colleagues around the country, another when he and his friend had been talking about this particular group. Ethan remembered a conversation on the conference call about logos and branding, and the issues that always cropped up when big organizations like the Y and the LIVE**STRONG** Foundation combined their looks and images to create a new brand. It was especially difficult for the Y, which had just introduced a new logo after almost thirty years with the old.

Brand compliance was a huge topic on its own. LIVE**STRONG** now needed to be written in capitals and with the "strong" bolded, because the foundation had adopted a new graphic standard and all new flyers, posters, and shirts had to adhere to it. The LIVE**STRONG** Foundation, it seemed, was trying to create an identity that was not solely dependent on the figurehead of Lance Armstrong—partly because of the doping scandal that was surrounding him and indeed always seemed to surround him in spite of the fact he had never failed a test, and partly because developing independence was thought to be a smart long-term plan.

But an offshoot of the branding conversation involved the yellow shirts. Some Y staff members were pressing for the new image, the specific logo for LIVE**STRONG** at the YMCA to be created, because their groups wanted to wear the yellow shirts—yellow, of course, being synonymous with Lance Armstrong, his exploits in the Tour de France, and now his foundation. Other staff had participants who did not want to wear the shirts, because it would make them stand out. They didn't want to be labeled by cancer, but instead wanted to exercise in a crowd, keeping the disease they had suffered a personal matter. Then there were YMCA staff who still wanted shirts even if their participants didn't, because they could sell them and raise funds for the program.

Ethan's group unanimously wanted shirts. For them, being involved in the LIVE**STRONG** at the YMCA program was a point of pride. In Sophie's opinion, they felt their efforts at the Y gave them inspiration and hope in their fight with cancer, along with a practical way to feel well and get well through exercise. They were also proud to be associated with the LIVE**STRONG** Foundation and with the Y that had provided a free opportunity for them to recover, and they wanted to announce that pride to all who could see or hear them.

Ethan had a shirt that Jenny had given him when he came to his first session, but it was at home in the back of his closet. As he watched the survivors working out, individually and together, he decided he would wear it the next time he came to exercise.

Each of the LIVE**STRONG** at the YMCA participants was engaged in their exercises, it seemed, in a different way. Some looked like Ethan, as though they were in the middle of an ordeal that caused grunts, groans, outright screams, and faces frozen with pain or contorted into ever-changing looks of dismay. Some were having fun, joking with partners or other members of the Y, smiling, laughing or focusing in a satisfied way as they tried to do things that were hard and often new to them. Looking around the room, it was clear that varied states of emotion and enjoyment were as common as sweat.

Many individuals who were not a part of the cancer survivor group seemed equally uncomfortable, struggling to do what they were doing, while others looked to be hurting, but in an accomplished way, absorbed and single-minded. Some were going through the motions gently, perhaps realizing or having been told by a Y staff member that they were beginning exercise for health reasons and so should not push themselves. They knew that the experience needed to be as painless as possible so that they would feel like returning to do more. Then there were those who were in the zone. They loved what they were doing and were almost ecstatic, competitive passion pulsing from their bodies as they pushed lungs and limbs to the limit.

As Ethan sat and recovered, Steve from the LIVE**STRONG** at the YMCA group spotted him and came over to say hello. He looked very at home in these surroundings, with a designer sheen of sweat on his brow. He was also clearly very relaxed with people, nodding and waving to folks as he crossed the wellness floor, then settling into conversation with his new friend as though he had known him for years.

"So, Ethan, you and Sophie have been buddies for a long time, yes?"

Ethan nodded and smiled.

"So you must know even more than I do about Y speak."

That made Ethan laugh out loud. The YMCA had many terms and sayings that were unique, because they saw themselves as unique, and these words or phrases would sneak their way into Sophie's vocabulary often, at which point he would put up his time-out hands and look for an explanation or definition. One example was the use of the term "wellness" instead of "fitness." The YMCA believed that many individuals were looking for ways to get well, and that wellness came in different forms. Becoming well could involve a variety of factors, including emotion and education, whereas becoming fit tended to involve the body. This explained why the YMCA was not a gym and only contained a gym if the particular facility had a basketball court. The exercise area was not a gym, but a wellness center. Gold's was a gym; Lifestyles was a gym; but the YMCA was the YMCA, with a different attitude and focus.

Steve wanted to talk about another term, and Ethan found it funny how he had launched into this topic with very little preamble. Perhaps he was trying to make a fellow survivor feel relaxed in a new environment surrounded by many strangers. Whatever it was, it seemed to be working.

"So talk to me about 'health seeker.' What on earth is a health seeker? All I hear in every corner of the Y, in every class I take, is the term 'health seeker.' Shoot, aren't we all health seekers?"

Ethan found the mock indignation Steve used to ask the question hilarious, and it made him laugh even harder. Eventually, though, he took a deep breath, leaned back in his chair, and tried to pass on the information he had gained with as much factual accuracy as possible.

"Okay, Steve, let's see if I was concentrating during one of Sophie's lectures. The YMCA realized relatively recently that as a charity and a family-focused organization, it was appealing to a group of the population that struggled to become healthy and struggled in their pursuit of wellness. It also realized that, since the nation as a whole was going through a healthcare crisis as the rate of obesity and related chronic diseases like diabetes rose alarmingly, it could best help the communities it served by focusing on that segment of the population."

Steve mimicked falling asleep on his feet, then laughed and punched Ethan in the shoulder. "Kidding, kidding. Go on."

Ethan gave him a pained look, then furrowed his brow in concentration. "While the Y had people who used their facilities who were fit and strong and found maintaining their health relatively easy, they had more individuals and families who found the whole path to wellness daunting and tough. They were people who had never exercised and now were suffering the consequences, or people who regularly started and then quickly stopped exercising because they found it hard. They were, as the YMCA now calls them, health seekers."

A round of applause greeted the end of the explanation. "Hey, Ethan, you listen well. Sophie needs to put you on the payroll."

Ethan was enjoying the conversation, but he was also playing for time a little. He prolonged the exercise break by pointing out the differences between his physical condition during exercise and Steve's. While he was sitting, breathing heavily and sweating after only ten minutes of biking, Steve looked as though he had just done a light warm-up and was ready to head off on a 10K.

Each man looked around the "wellness center" and saw health seekers everywhere. Of course, they could not label everyone, because many had struggles that manifested themselves internally; but other signs were clear, including pain, uncertainty, and sometimes just plain fear on faces, and of course bodies that were deconditioned or overweight.

"Steve, I've been a health seeker all my life. I always wanted to be good at sports, but I wasn't, so I didn't play. I was forced to be involved in a sport, but I hated it, and at the first opportunity, I stopped doing it. I found a form of exercise I liked, biking, but I started and stopped throughout my life because of work, social commitments, and laziness. And of course, now I have cancer. As a cancer survivor, maybe I'm the ultimate health seeker."

Ethan's new friend looked at him with a big smile and held out his hand to shake. "Okay, buddy, now I know what a health seeker is, and it sounds like I'm one, too. Want to help each other through this?"

9

Sophie loved her work and loved the impact her YMCA had on the community and individuals in the community. She was particularly proud at the moment, though, because a program she worked on nationally was making a difference locally, in her own Y.

LIVE**STRONG** at the YMCA had ingrained itself in her heart, as she saw the program grow and as she saw the cancer survivors affected by the initiative thrive. Currently that passion was reaching a peak, as she continued to work on a national gathering of colleagues involved with this effort and as she continued to see signs of progress in members that she had come to know personally.

Sophie was a YMCA lifer. She had grown up in Dallas and had learned to swim, play soccer and basketball, and do her first handspring, all at the Plano Y. She had just started with the Leaders Club there when she had moved to Detroit with her family, and leaving that Y, her friends, and the staff she had grown up with had been nearly as difficult as leaving her school and classmates.

But Detroit, while hard to get used to in many ways, turned out to be a good fit, in large part because of the YMCA. Her family had joined a local branch called Lakeshore that was only ten minutes from their home, and they often visited Downtown, a Y that was a little farther away but bigger.

Sophie's father worked at the Henry Ford Medical Center. He was very philanthropic, and a proponent of non-profits that worked in the heart of communities that had great need. He was a very large donor to the Detroit YMCA and made a point of explaining why to Sophie, and whenever possible, he also made a point of taking her on any donor tours or visits he was asked to make to Y branches or program sites.

Sophie always enjoyed hearing Ethan talk about his first impression of the Y as two big, old, imposing buildings that served the homeless. She had moved to Detroit in the late seventies and had also been immediately amazed at the diversity of folks that used the Downtown branch in particular. It was nine stories tall, comprising mostly resident rooms and facilities, and housed the homeless, poor workers, and travelers, in addition to acting as a halfway house for recently released felons.

But the Y also provided wellness options for a large number of workers who commuted into the city, including some high-end businesspeople who enjoyed the basement pool, racquetball courts, and steam room. On any given day, visitors might see a steady stream of African-American and Caucasian men and women going into and out of the front doors of the Y—some with no shoes, some with three-piece suits, and some with a gym bag, lunch pail, and hard hat under their arm.

Sometimes, her father would buy her lunch from American Coney Island, and they would sit on a bench just to watch the comings and goings from the Y.

"Sophie, do you know why I give money to this Y?"

She would shake her head, even though he asked the question with great regularity and she knew the answer.

"It's because it is a quintessential social gathering place. It has something for everyone—old or young, black or white, rich or poor."

"And why is that important, Dad? Why is it important to you?"

Like many daughters, Sophie was never so happy as when she had the attention of her hard-working father.

"Because we are all becoming more and more isolated, Sophie, focused inward rather than outward. There are limited options for gathering, or at least healthy gathering, and the Y provides that for all levels of society. Where else would you find this?" He pointed to the front doors of the Y. "Not even church."

Sophie often thought of those visits to the Detroit YMCA and her father's support of the YMCA organization as a whole. His views had influenced her career choice and if he were with her, in Florida, she could picture him talking in the same way, with the same level of passion, about her current workplace. The Palm Harbor YMCA was also a gathering place, and with the facility's implementation of LIVE**STRONG** at the YMCA and other chronic disease programs, its diversity lay in the health of the individuals that became members, rather than in their race or social standing. That was really what made YMCA cancer survivor efforts so successful around the country—the results that came from exercise, for sure, but also the opportunity for folks to gather.

Norma alluded to this in a group discussion one day, and people nodded in agreement left and right. "Sophie, there came a point when I was as sick of being in a medical environment as I was sick of cancer. Coming to the Y was like stepping outside on a sunny day. I can exercise, but I also get to talk, live, and laugh with my cancer survivor friends and with regular Y folks, too, all in a 'normal' setting."

So Sophie was extremely proud. She would have been prouder still if her best friend would immerse himself in all aspects of LIVE**STRONG** at the YMCA. She knew that Ethan was trying hard to come to terms with his illness, and trying hard to commit to the cancer survivor exercise program. He had in fact made inroads, taking a wellness consultation with Jenny and getting to know Steve a little better. But it was clear he was struggling with many physical and mental aspects of his disease, and while there were similarities between Ethan and his fellow survivors and the barriers they faced, his road was also very personal. She knew all she could do was listen and be supportive, but she also wondered, more than she wondered with any other survivor with whom she'd worked, was there something else she should be doing?

10

Super Bowl Sunday involved rituals, especially when the New England Patriots and Tom Brady were on the field—but for Ethan, there were some unique challenges for this, the 2012 game. Generally, the prospect of seeing speed, skill, and brutality in many guises, dripping with sweat and accompanied by a ferocious desire to win—all part of a package that was the biggest game of the year—was enough to engross and excite him. But this year, the pre-game analysis just didn't entertain him as much—mainly because he could not stay comfortable on the couch in front of the television.

That morning had been an early one for Ethan. After a little sleep and lots of rolling around and fidgeting, he had gotten up to greet Jay—who was ready and eager for anything, twenty-four hours a day—and they had gone for a long walk in the dark. Along the way, his dog had found many wonders without needing daylight, discovering scents in every bush and crevice. They wandered streets and avenues with no destination in mind, though Ethan knew that eventually they would end up back home, courtesy of Jay's nose and sixth sense.

Unlike Jay, Ethan relied on his eyes to find wonders. Taking his eyes off the road, he gazed up into a cloudless, deep, black Floridian sky rife with stars and planets, perhaps even galaxies—who knew what they were, but they were beautiful and everywhere, in all directions. He could look up and lose himself in creation, leap upward, dazzled and lost, past other worlds and beings—all the while knowing that, back on Planet Earth, his dog would guide his troubled mind and body safely around cars and corners as they walked.

Ethan was tired and walking early because his treatments were still causing him discomfort—a lot of discomfort. He was taking chemo orally and had started getting mouth sores. This annoyance, small in the scheme of things, was still irritating and debilitating. He didn't have much of an appetite anyway, and because of the pain in his mouth, he now lacked the ability and desire to eat. All of these side effects and the constant, throbbing knowledge that he had cancer meant that Ethan often felt depressed, anti-social, and sorry for himself. Even though these feelings were repugnant, it was tough to break the cycle.

That said, he was discovering at last that there were areas of his psyche that were more robust than others, particularly when it came to Sophie. There was obviously some deeper instinct at play with his friend, some trigger that kicked out the chemicals that forced him to adopt a level of masculine protectiveness, because he absolutely did not want to upset or concern her any more than she already was.

So Ethan was still determinedly going to the LIVE**STRONG** at the YMCA sessions, predominantly because it made Sophie happy. That was also why, when he was with her having lunch or dinner and she worried about him getting thin, he ate, when the last thing he wanted to do was eat, drank when the last thing he wanted to do was drink, and conversed when often all he wanted to do was go to bed. Sophie didn't know that he had mouth sores or that he was having trouble with diarrhea. She did know that he was feeling nauseated and throwing up, and she did know he was losing his hair, because it was hard to hide those symptoms. But Ethan could keep some things hidden, and when he did, it made him feel perversely good inside.

From a purely football perspective, 2012 was shaping up to have a better Super Bowl day than previous years. Ethan didn't feel as nervous as he had when Tom Brady had played in the past, maybe because, at last, he had heard the message that sports fans and analysts had been pounding out for years: Tom Brady supporters had no reason to be nervous, because he was that good.

But Ethan considered himself an above-average armchair football analyst and psychologist, and he had a theory that one of the greatest quarterbacks of all time did suffer from stress at certain times in a game. One of the reasons he liked Tom Brady was because he had been very underrated in his youth. He'd come to the University of Michigan as a second-string starter to Drew Henson, who was a baseball and football prodigy, but Brady had done well regardless and won some big games for the school. He was then drafted into the NFL as a sixth-round pick, having been passed over by many teams before being plucked out of obscurity by Bill Belichick as a backup to Drew Bledsoe. Bledsoe had gotten injured; Brady won the 2002 Super Bowl, became one of the most talked about and admired players in the game, and the rest was history. Still, there was a boulder-sized chip on his shoulder.

Ethan's theory was that this chip had helped Brady many times because it drove him to excel, but he also thought it had an opposite effect at key moments in some games, an effect that made this record-breaking quarterback second-guess whether he really did belong at such a high level. He thought this had become more evident as Brady got older, as his skills and instincts failed to get him out of the jams he once had avoided. It was a theory that he kept to himself, because to the average football observer, it was pretty crazy. But recent statistics didn't lie. Brady had great regular season numbers, but no Super Bowl ring since 2005.

Theory or not, Ethan still wanted him to win. He thought there was a level of arrogance in his walk and talk, and in spite of that, or maybe because of it, he liked him. As a three-time world champion with a supermodel wife, perhaps he deserved to have some arrogance. And there was a purely selfish reason Ethan wanted him to win: there was something about having spotted early, and then supported long-term, one of the greatest quarterbacks of all time, and Brady needed one more championship victory under his belt to be talked about in those circles.

So why was Ethan not nervous this time, when he had been so edgy and uptight in the past? Sophie thought the answer was obvious. She couldn't imagine anyone suffering from cancer being nervous about a game. A team was going to win and a team was going to lose, but all of the players involved would be on vacation the next day, relatively carefree.

And perhaps Sophie was right. Ethan had just had what was probably a stage three or four cancerous tumor removed and he was still waiting for the final results of that operation to see if it was successful. A football game, even a world championship, did pale next to that.

His friend also repeated her favorite mantra: if Brady won another Super Bowl, great; but if he didn't, he still had millions of dollars in the bank, a ridiculously beautiful and successful wife by his side, and career accomplishments that belied his status as a sixth-round draft pick. Drew Henson was working in an office as a financial manager for professional athletes, while Tom Brady was a professional athlete playing in perhaps the biggest game on the planet in front of millions of adoring fans. Maybe Sophie was right. What was there to be nervous about?

But, nerves or no nerves, the superstar lost again. In Ethan's opinion, he'd had the game in his grasp and had literally thrown it away. When a quarterback of that stature had the ball with five or six minutes remaining and his team was winning, skill, flair, innovation, tenacity, drive—the ingredients that had made Tom Brady a thoroughbred among pack horses—should have also made the difference. But they didn't. One of the ingredients was missing.

Sophie always made vegetarian Super Bowl chili on the big day, and it was always so good. Most often, she made it at her house for her friends and neighbors, but this time she came around to Ethan's house. This year he couldn't taste the chili very well. The spices set his mouth sores on fire and made him feel nauseated, but he ate a whole bowl, smiled, and helped clean up. Tom Brady may have lost, but Sophie was right—there were more important things in life, and friendship was one of them.

11

Ethan had a preferred Florida relaxation spot, his favorite place to sit in the sun and contemplate living in paradise. Honeymoon Island was a picturesque little landmass just off the Dunedin coastline, attached by a short causeway. It was a state park and had some of the most beautiful beaches in the country. It had been formed in 1921, when a hurricane separated it from the smaller Caladesi Island, leaving two natural areas for locals and tourists alike to enjoy.

Ethan used to go the island regularly to swim, walk trails, and lounge on the beaches, which were quieter than Clearwater's—but post-cancer, he came more to sit, sun himself, and watch his dog play in the park. Dogs, in his mind, were as smart as dog owners thought they were. He believed his Lab had a sense of who he was and where he was, and had as many likes and dislikes as his owner. His favorite dog food was Pedigree (he had no time for generic brands), and he liked snacking on vegetables when Ethan made lunch or dinner and employed the one-for-you-and-one-for-me method of cooking. He adored Sophie but was jealous if she ever visited with a friend, and Honeymoon Island was his absolute favorite dog park. Not only could he run, sniff, and play with friends new and old; he could also swim and romp around on a canine-only beach. Every trip to the island was a mini-vacation.

On this particular day, while Ethan sat on a bench with a bottle of water, a book, and an umbrella for shade, Jay alternated between chasing seagulls in all directions and sleeping at his owner's feet. His actual name was Jayzee: he had been named after the rapper because of his dark good looks and his tendency to howl as a puppy when he heard the "Life and Times of S. Carter" at full volume. But for everyday use, "Jay" worked fine.

Ethan had Detroit and his parents on his mind. The Motor City was in his thoughts because he had watched basketball on TNT the night before, and the Pistons had been playing the Knicks. Beautiful beaches and sunshine should have drawn his attention back to the here and now, and a nice breeze and warmth should have relaxed him, but there was something about his hometown that tugged. He resisted for a while, but after admiring the view, breathing in the sea air, and watching a couple of fishermen wading out into the shallows to cast, the allure of Detroit sucked him back in: the game first, then the city, and then his parents. The game was fresh; he could still picture the swagger and sweat. Memories of his parents and the city were not fresh, but they were never far from his thoughts.

Last night's contest had been fun to watch because of the skill and athleticism on display, but also because the game had been held at the Palace of Auburn Hills, home of Detroit basketball and a location Ethan had visited often in the past. In fact, he had been there for the first-ever game played when it opened for the 1988–89 season, courtesy of his little article on the phantom pass and his relationship with Fat-Fingered Tony.

Ethan had been given a press pass allowing him to go to the opening ceremonies and the game, which, to a sports-loving college student, was like being given a bag of gold. He even got to visit Tony, briefly, while the man watched the game from a private box as a guest of Coleman Young, the Detroit mayor at that time. It was a big deal to see Young in an environment that suited his reputation: surrounded by influential friends in a luxury box and drinking the finest wines while eating the finest food. Mr. Young had been the first-ever African-American mayor of Detroit, and unfortunately one of the most corrupt. Millions of dreams lived with Coleman Young for a long time, and he ripped them apart and chewed them up like peanuts at a basketball game.

It was a roundabout route, but the Pistons took Ethan's mind to Detroit; Detroit took his mind to Coleman Young; and the former mayor reminded him of his parents because, unfortunately, they were both extremely insensitive when it came to race. His dad was the worst; he was too often a mean, angry bigot. His mother? While it was hard to make excuses for anyone who discriminated, Ethan just thought his mother had come of age in the wrong environment and didn't know any better.

Both of his parents had been raised by Southern-born families that had moved to Detroit during the latter part of the boom years when the city was humming, creating machinery for the war effort in the 1940s. Ethan's dad was a numbers man, good at mathematics and science, and he put himself through college while working construction. He married straight out of school, when he was still a lower level accountant in the Ford finance department, had put a roof over the heads of his wife and three kids by buying a falling-down old boarding house in Wyandotte. He was then plucked out of the accountant masses to help with a startup pizza company that was expanding by leaps and bounds. That start-up later became Domino's.

The prospects were good, the money was good, but whether the success had gone to his dad's head or whether his father possessed an innate meanness that just continued to grow, Ethan never knew. All he knew was that his family hardly had a male role model in the house during the early seventies because that role model generally bypassed his home after work to hit the local bars and clubs. He would appear to his children in sound only, at midnight or one or two o'clock, cursing and shouting and occasionally hitting his wife while the kids pulled blankets over their heads in an adjacent room and tried to sleep and dream.

Ethan was not sure how his mother had ever convinced her good-for-nothing, drunken husband to spend some of his hard-earned money to move everyone to Royal Oak, but she had, and it was like going to sleep in Detroit and waking up in Disneyland. Maybe the decision to move had been linked to his father's desire to leave the family; maybe there was an ounce of goodness in him, and when he'd seen his kids playing in a fenced, green-grass yard or biking safely down a leaf-strewn road, he'd thought it was finally okay to abandon them.

"Abandon" was the right word: Ethan's father had left without a word of explanation or a wave goodbye. Ethan remembered being emotionally torn when that happened. His memories of his dad were memories of anger: sounds of rage at night, his mom's bruised face, tones of fury as his father railed against black Detroit and the city's newly installed black leadership, drunken altercations with neighbors. The only positive images Ethan had of this fearsome man were ones of him plunging into the water, his distant head bobbing and pulling away from the pack, emerging to sail past with precise speed on a highly tuned and desirable bike before resorting to his legs to pound along one gray city street or another, finishing first, second, or third; he was one of the best triathletes in the city, which so belied his hard-drinking, fast-food-eating, unhealthy persona.

Even that positive image of him as an athlete had been tarnished when he got into a fight with a black competitor at the finish line of the Chrysler Super Tri, after the man had had the audacity to run him close in the race.

Ethan had gone up to visit his parents when he was first diagnosed with cancer because he felt he owed them some closeness, some face time. He wanted to explain what was going on and provide them with some reassurance, although he did not feel reassured himself. His mom needed the comfort; she had been an emotional wreck on the phone when Ethan told her the news, and she was the same in person.

He walked along the familiar pathway that led to his old house in Royal Oak. It was still leaf-strewn, the perfect bike track for a six-year-old, and the nostalgia felt warm for a moment. But then it turned cold as he saw his sobbing mother at the end of the driveway, waiting to hug the sickness out of her child.

After the initial emotion had passed and he had spent time sitting and talking with his mom, Ethan realized that on the surface she was doing well. She had a part-time job as an administrative assistant at a high school and received money from his dad and all of her kids. She fussed, made coffee, talked about his brother and sister and then her friends. She told him how the economy had really hit the city hard and then, as though his health were somehow linked to the health of Detroit, she brought the conversation back around to her oldest son and cancer.

It was easy to calm her—cancer always sounds bad at first and over the phone—but after she had seen her child and made sure he had not wasted away physically or emotionally, she was able to take a deep breath and smile.

Both of Ethan's siblings lived nearby, and they made plans to go out for dinner that evening. His sister was down in Toledo and worked for Fifth Third Bank as a corporate account manager. When he talked to her on the phone she also seemed content: she had married well and had two boys in their teens. His brother lived in Ann Arbor and was an information technology specialist for the University of Michigan. He had always been a tech geek and was in heaven helping to make such a huge organization hum, especially when that organization was the fabled Wolverines. Ethan could imagine his brother whistling the Michigan fight song at his desk as he manipulated software and hardware. He had also married well, to a professor who worked for the University of Michigan's social science department. They had three children, two girls and a boy.

As Ethan and his mother sat in her house and drank tea, it was as easy as ever—perhaps easier with cancer hovering—for Ethan's mom to steer the conversation around to his status as a single man. She felt there was still time for him to meet someone, still time to get married, still time for him to have kids; and by the way, how was that lovely girl Sophie? As she talked, probed, and worried, she fell sound asleep in her armchair, snoring lightly, looking at peace with the world at last after the stress of thinking about her sickly son. Ethan was exhausted after traveling all morning, and of course because of his illness, but with his mom sleeping, he decided to take the opportunity to quietly look around and remember.

The house was now much too big for her. It had three bedrooms and two bathrooms upstairs; and two bedrooms, a bathroom, a dining room, a kitchen, and a big living room downstairs. Then there was a full basement, which had once been a play area. The main floor was in good shape—relatively clean and tidy—but when Ethan climbed the stairs, he found an old, unkempt museum. It was as if the children still lived in the house. No one had dusted for years and time had come to a halt in the 1980s.

In one room, his brother's Tigers pennants and posters still covered the walls, and an old bat signed by Kirk Gibson held a place of pride on a dresser. Group photos of his brother with teammates were everywhere; he had been a good ballplayer in his day, a third baseman and solid slugger.

Ethan's sister's room honored her high school days, with yearbooks on display, a prom dress hanging behind the door, and photos of her and various classmates on the walls, in frames, lying on the dressing table and bedside counters. Many of the faces had no meaning to him anymore, but he could recognize the regulars, friends that had visited often and been solid companions for his sister throughout school. Mary Sullivan, Jill Dankowski, Patty Roberts, Kelly Hubert—all of them stared out through a film of dust, smiling and young.

Ethan had to sit down and soak in his own room, breathing in the angst, then closing his eyes to smell it, too, sifting through memories in his mind. There were posters of Isiah Thomas and Joe Dumars from the Pistons on one wall, and Jim Harbaugh and Bo Schembechler from Michigan on the other. His mom had framed every *Free Press* article ever published under Ethan's byline: his Phantom Foul highlight, a report on a hardware store shooting and the lives that had been ruined, a story about a white boy and his rescue dog who had pulled a homeless black man from the Detroit River. The paper and print were fading despite the glass protection, but Ethan could still read the words, and did read every one.

His room was unique because of the absence of photographs. There were no images of himself or friends. As he sat there, he tried to remember people who had been in his classes or with whom he'd graduated, and while a few names came to mind, there weren't many.

Ethan's room was also exceptional because it was the cleanest, as though his Mom had decided that dusting and vacuuming might also wash away her son's disease. It was a sterile bedroom, neat, tidy, and faceless, and the air held a vague scent of lemons.

The most disconcerting area of the house in terms of his mother, however, was the basement. Ethan wasn't sure why he went down there to snoop, but he soon wished he hadn't. The door barely opened, blocked by a stack of boxes. When he pulled on the light switch, all he could see were piles of old books and fabric, stacks of newspapers, and old toys and games. When he sniffed the air, it smelled musty and stale. His mom had always been a hoarder—she hated to throw things away, and she used all manner of things to sustain the family. What was she hoarding for now, though? The grandkids, perhaps—but it seemed like the basement had not been visited for a long time, as though the stockpiling had continued for years even as the using had dried up.

Ethan kept quiet about his tour of the house when his mom woke up. He was there, in the same chair, reading a book when she opened her eyes and smiled, confused a little as to what time it was and who was there. They had more tea and he left her to visit his dad, knowing they would be back together for dinner the same evening.

Like any child, he found it hard to grasp the aging process and had no ability to attribute age to the adults who had raised and cared for him. But clearly his mom was overwhelmed with her house, lonely perhaps, and heading down a road that would only get darker and more challenging if she was not helped. Ethan was ashamed that it had taken cancer to bring him home to see his mother's pain, and that cancer might stop him from making up for lost time.

He wondered at her lack of friends, wondered if she had ever had friends or if the family, especially the single-parent family, had been all-consuming. He also assumed now that her frequent get-togethers with his brother, sister, and the grandkids were all one-way visits; she must travel there and have no one out to her house. As he drove deeper into Detroit, Ethan called his brother to see what they could do to help collectively.

His dad had been surprised to hear from his oldest son, perhaps because they had not spoken in over a decade. He took the cancer announcement in his stride and then seemed wary and nervous at the suggestion that they get together. That could have been Ethan's interpretation of the conversation, which had been a brief two minutes worth of small talk, but he was glad they had settled on a mid-afternoon drink, which meant tea or coffee in his mind.

They met at Nemo's because it was common ground. Ethan's dad had always been a hockey fan, enjoyed the physical nature of the game, the fights more than the skill. One of the first things he proudly told his son when they sat down to meet was that he still came to Nemo's before home games, which meant he caught that same shuttle bus that Sophie and Ethan had taken years before. That was perhaps the most revealing part of their conversation, the most personal at least; his father still liked to watch men fight.

He was a faded patriarch, old and tired, and as they sat at the bar, at four o'clock in the afternoon, he had a beer and a shot—a pick-me-up that was usual for that time of day, Ethan thought. He asked a number of questions about his father's life, but the responses were muted, guarded, as though the man suspected the meeting and Ethan's cancer were a trap, as though he expected a catch coming somewhere in the conversation. Ethan tried to figure out what a trap might look like to his father—money or friendship, maybe reconciliation in the face of death. The meeting was uncomfortable, short, and ended with a formal handshake and no smiles.

As he watched his dad walk away to his car, a made-in-Detroit Dodge Charger, Ethan experienced again that uncomfortable understanding that he was stronger than his parents, and indeed perhaps now responsible for his parents. His father had a very prominent belly and a limp, and he seemed angry still, though now with a little more sadness mixed in. He had not once asked how his son was feeling, how he was coping. What would Ethan's reaction have been if his dad had said, "Tell me about your illness, son"? He was not sure he would have shared. He was older, stronger, more responsible; but he was a child with cancer, a child that could have used some parental love.

He did not bring up any of his observations about his father when the family had dinner that night. The focus at first was his cancer and how he was doing, and then it shifted to home lives and most especially to the grandkids. Ethan's mother shone in those surroundings, and it was obvious that she was proud of her own children and happy that her family had grown. The spotlight never switched to her, had never been on her, and all involved left it that way because she didn't like the spotlight.

Maybe a phone call at another time would be a good idea. Ethan could ask questions, probe a little into her plans, and nudge her to move out of that old house. He lived far away and perhaps it was not his business anymore, but the clean lemon smell in his old room said he needed to make it his business. His mom still cared for her oldest son, even cleaned for him, and he needed to start caring for her.

It was Jay who brought Ethan out of his daydream on Honeymoon Island, standing, stretching, and releasing a long, hungry moan. He was getting antsy, and his owner was beginning to feel so tired that it would be hard to drive if he didn't leave straight away. Ethan made a note, though, to call his mother that night to see how she was doing and to reassure her that he was well.

12

All of Ethan's negative feelings and fears collided the morning he received a call from his doctor. It was time to come back in for tests to determine how successful the operation and chemo pills had been. The thought of knowing did not bring a sense of opportunity, or a chance for relief, however—just a sense of dread. Unfortunately, in his mind, a physician was not a healer but a harbinger of doom, and Ethan's psyche continued to be brittle. Why he was so ill-equipped for this ordeal, so fragile, he didn't know.

His father had risen from construction worker to the business engine of a startup company to the global executive of a financial investment firm. He was extremely successful, brimming with confidence in his abilities, but also highly flawed as a person. His mother had always been a part-time worker and constant caregiver, also very successful, as evidenced by her three great kids—but she was troubled, too. She had held her family together with a smile fraying at the edges, and was now lonely and sad at a time when she should have been celebrating her accomplishments. Neither of them had ever shown outward signs of weakness until the aging process had robbed them of that veneer that parents have. Ethan did not have a veneer, had never had a veneer—but face-to-face with cancer, he suddenly needed a mask, one that he could curl up behind, to hide.

Was it a guy thing to relate everything back to sports, to find strength in physical feats of prowess and competition? Yes, and Ethan was no different, even though he had not excelled in sports. Afraid, head in hands, he thought if he could be as cool as Tom Brady, everything would be okay, even though just a few nights ago he had been questioning Tom Brady's ability. What about, if he was as cool as Michael Jordan, everything would be okay? If an individual had the confidence to throw a good pass or catch a good pass or drop in a three-point shot under pressure, would he or she then have the ability to look cancer in the eye and say, "I can take you, Big C"? Lance was, of course, a better example, the Michael Jordan of the cycling world, the Tom Brady of the peloton. Success bred success; confidence bred confidence; will to win bred will to win.

But Ethan had never thrown or caught a pass under pressure, or hit a mid-range jump shot as the clock ticked down; he was never quite good enough to be put in those situations. He had just run a lot of laps on a cold, windy track in Michigan, a lot of unfocused, unhappy, "let's just get this over with" laps. Now he had continuous thoughts of cancer pounding in his mind like a pair of Nikes on pavement: his tests, the "what ifs" of those tests, the "what now" after those tests.

Later in the day, after the phone call, Ethan had gone to the Y to join his group in exercise, but it had been a mistake to think he could interact in any way with others. Fear had driven him away from his session without saying goodbye to anyone, had driven him to a coffee house so he could flick through magazines without seeing the words or pictures. What if he had the tests and went back to the doctor and the results were positive? He had lived through a six-pound tumor being removed from his insides and he was now taking poison twice a day. What if it were all to no avail? What if he died? What the hell had he done with his life?

There were many reasons why Ethan followed cycling and looked to biking as his main source of fitness. He had fond memories of watching his dad ride a really nice Gitane bike in Detroit, mainly during triathlons but also in other road races. As much as he had disliked his dad, it was funny how affectionate his memories of him on that bike were. It was this family connection and admiration for cycling that made Ethan a Tour de France fan. He remembered watching Greg LeMond win the first of his three Tours in 1986 and then being even more enraptured when he won again in

1989 and 1990. After that, Ethan had made a point of developing his own little routine around the Tour, eating a baguette and Camembert cheese at the start of the race every year, and toasting the final procession down the Champs-Élysées with champagne.

And then came Lance Armstrong; he took Ethan's love and fascination for the event and the sport to a new level. When Lance won his first tour and then embarked on an amazing run that captured the next six events, Ethan was in awe, every year in awe, until, when Armstrong won his seventh and final race, Ethan was not sipping champagne but was drunk on the stuff, giddy with excitement and admiration. At the time, he was not so much caught up in the "victor who had recovered from cancer" story line. It was just the winning, then winning again, and then Lance becoming the greatest cyclist of all time. Ethan had read an article in the *New York Times* that analyzed the race and it said,

> The Tour de France is arguably the most physiologically demanding of athletic events. The effort has been compared to running a marathon several days a week for nearly three weeks, while the total elevation of the climbs has been compared to climbing three Everests.

For Ethan, that was the thing about watching Lance as opposed to Tom: it really never seemed like Lance would lose, and it especially never seemed like Lance would lose when the weight of the world was on his back. Race, reputation, history—it meant nothing compared to the sheer joy of winning. When Ethan looked at Lance, he saw steely eyes; with Tom, Ethan saw the same steely eyes, but also a small tic in one cheek.

But how did one manufacture steel when steel was needed? Ethan wanted to be as strong, as focused, as sure of himself and the outcome of his fight as Lance had been—but he just did not know where that mental makeup came from, did not think it could be dredged up from the depths of a will that was shallow. In the coffee shop, he kept thinking as he pretended to read, flipping pages in old editions of *Sports Illustrated* and meaningless copies of *People* magazine. He kept pausing to put his head in his hands, to try to steady the bouts of panic and nausea that were bubbling to the surface. He was trying to think of something to focus on, something that could diminish the importance of cancer, the threat of cancer—and it was shameful that he couldn't. He had Sophie and Jay, and his mom perhaps—a friend, a dog, and a parent, nothing deeper than that.

Sophie turned up in the coffee shop, and she wore anger and sadness intermingled on her face. She also seemed exasperated and confused, which meant she was a cacophony of emotions as she sat opposite Ethan and stared into his eyes. She was not herself. The dual life she had been living as a LIVE**STRONG** at the YMCA staff member and as Ethan's close friend, the facade that had made it seem as though she were okay with both roles, had blown away in the wind as she traveled from the Y to the coffee house.

"What's going on?" She was definitely not listen-first Sophie.

"I have to go for tests. It's time."

That brought a deep breath and a softer expression. "How does that make you feel?"

"Scared. Lonely."

"Is there something you can do, do you think, that might ease the fright, ease the loneliness?"

Ethan just sat in silence, looking down, even though Sophie gave him ample time to answer. So she spoke again.

"Ethan, I'm really trying hard not to see two of you, I promise. Some days I see a friend who has cancer, and other days I see a cancer survivor who is a friend. Trouble is, I think I would treat each of you differently."

"It's just me, Sophie. Same old me, just a little sicker." His hands were tight together on the table, fingers interlocking, close to prayer.

"Okay, what I should be doing is more listening, I know, but it's hard. So let me just talk to the friend and put my profession aside. I think you are trying; I've been very impressed by how much you're trying, but you're focusing on yourself too much, your own illness too much. I think if you start looking around at others and the troubles they have, and the ways in which they are overcoming their troubles, or struggling with their troubles, maybe you might find hope, or inspiration, or maybe cause. And maybe you could share, too, give some hope to others who need it."

Ethan couldn't stop a tear from welling in one eye, rolling down his cheek, and dropping squarely into the center of an empty cup. Sophie's head bowed momentarily, and then she took a breath and carried on.

"Ethan, other than the cancer, what is it that makes you feel so negative about yourself at the moment?"

No response.

"I love your writing. You have such a talent, but it is definitely interspersed with sadness, inner frustrations, as much darkness as light." She paused again, thinking. "Is there something you could do differently that might change the way you feel, make it easier to think positively?"

"I could find out I'm cancer-free."

They both smiled, even though there was a bare minimum of humor in the statement.

"What about making friends, really making friends with people, deepening your relationships? What about opening yourself up, making yourself a little vulnerable? Allowing people inside might help you connect on the outside. People really do like you, I just don't think they know you."

Ethan was not reacting verbally, but Sophie could see her words having an effect on him physically: she just didn't know if the effect was good or bad.

She reached out and put her hand on his cheek. "I love you, Ethan. You're my best friend. I have to say again that I know you're trying, but I think you might be able to try harder. Open up! Be *you*, instead of half of you, and then you might find the strength you need to get through this."

He was crying softly now, elbows on the table, head in his hands. "It's cancer, Sophie. It doesn't matter who I am. I have cancer, the great indiscriminate disease."

"It does matter who you are, and it does matter how you act, what you do, how you fight. Ethan, you are a good, caring, talented, gay cancer survivor. I really think being who you are will give you strength—and being who you are will give others strength, too."

13

Ethan was walking around his house haphazardly, absorbed; and this bemused his dog. Jayzee followed him everywhere expectantly, detecting a sense of purpose in the air, though the purpose was accompanied by random meandering from room to room. Eventually, as his energy stores dried up, Ethan tried some gentle exercises and realized that he had no flexibility in his body at all, and that he needed to ask Jenny about stretching.

Interestingly, the whole discussion with Sophie had—eventually—caused a release of mental tension. He had a scan planned for the end of the week, but was too busy thinking to be scared, too busy contemplating and speculating, because there were many layers to Sophie's appeal. The concrete ball in his stomach, the tunnel vision zeroing in on his tests, and in particular, the feared bad results of his tests—all were gone for the time being. Instead he was pondering.

Sophie had been very convincing. She had seemed genuinely emotional, as she always was when she saw Ethan struggling with the effects of cancer, but there was also a calculating glimmer in her eyes. The expression on her face held elements of determination and focus that felt like they had been fermenting, bubbling under the surface, and were now finally combining to produce a meaningful, directed intent. She was emotional about the way her friend was handling his cancer diagnosis, but also eager to force him into submission regarding his sexuality.

So in his house Ethan stretched and drank green tea instead of coffee and thought about all of the things she had said. He imagined he was being holistic as he deliberated, trying new and natural things to become focused, and that green tea and stretching might equal yoga and karmic peace, acceptance of fate.

Ethan thought there was a lot of validity to Sophie's opinion that he was being selfish. She hadn't used the word "selfish," because that would have been anathema to her as a Y professional, but the underlying meaning was clear. His own fears were definitely inward looking. He had been unable to talk to other survivors in his group, unable to sympathize, empathize, listen or help in any way. The majority of his consciousness had been focused on himself and his own sickness. He could not stop thinking "why me?" and he could not stop thinking that he was not going to beat this thing, even as others were opening up to individuals or to the group, trying to help themselves and help friends. To not be concentrating, listening, when other people, other survivors, were revealing their vulnerabilities, when they were looking for support—the more Ethan thought of how he had acted, the more disappointed he became, and the more he understood that Sophie was right. He needed to take a breath; he needed to help and be helped.

There was also much truth to her observation that he was not making friends, had not made friends in Florida, and really, had not nurtured or maintained many friendships in his lifetime. During his time in Palm Harbor, it had always been easy to blame a lack of time, his job, his house, or his dog for his inability to develop relationships, even though there were people at work who were interesting and fun to be with, people he should have been trying harder to connect with and to understand on a more personal level. In Detroit, as a child and later in adulthood, he had found it hard to open a door to his heart, to give and receive trust completely, for various reasons—and without trust, true connections are rarely made.

In the last couple of years, on more and more occasions, he had often felt a sense of tiredness at the end of the working day, and sitting and shutting off often seemed preferable to socializing. Ethan had felt this way even before cancer, felt like sharing this life involved expending too much energy when that energy had been drained by humdrum hours in an office.

Was he tired or uninspired—unable to picture the joy that might come from relationships built and emotions shared, because he spent his days in a pleasure vacuum? He was conscious of the duality of his work-life as he analyzed it—his employers and colleagues were kind and warm, but the work itself was like sitting in a bucket of ice for a day: harsh and cold, draining the heat from his life.

He was not like Sophie and the Y. Accounting and financial advising were not his life, and frankly, it felt good to leave it behind—but did he need to leave everything about it behind, even the people? And if accounting was not his life, then what was? He had been out of school for more than twenty years, and time had passed by in a flash; so what was his reason for being?

Ethan sat at last—much to Jay's relief—so that he could focus on Sophie's main point. Did he need to come to terms with his own sexuality to beat cancer, or, at the very least, might it help? His love life—or lack of it—was one of the few areas where he consistently disagreed with his friend. She found great joy in being an open book in all areas of life, and certainly regarding her sexuality and femininity. She was a flirt who knew who she was and was happy to let everyone else know who she was. She was pretty, funny, and smart, and all of that, packaged in a fit, strong body, made her gorgeous.

They had known each other for about a week when Sophie asked Ethan if he was gay, and after only knowing her for that week, he told her something he had kept to himself for many, many years. That was another piece of the package that Sophie had—or rather, the ribbon and bow on the package, because she was instantly trustworthy. That was what made her such a good staff member at the Y and the perfect candidate to oversee the LIVE**STRONG** at the YMCA program, to work with cancer survivors. When a person was sitting and talking to Sophie, it didn't matter if they were vulnerable in any way. If that person looked her in the eye and held out his or her heart, that heart was safe.

After a week as friends, she had boldly told Ethan that he had not made any kind of move on her and so must be gay. It would have been easy to laugh that comment off, to jab back at her for being so sure of herself, full of herself. But he'd experienced that same rush of blood that had made him talk to her at the hockey game, had thought then and there how refreshing it would be to be honest—and so he was honest, and said yes, he was gay.

She didn't understand why he could not admit this to the whole world, why he could not just be himself. She thought it was like getting a new haircut or a new shirt: just do it, and eventually the stares would stop, or, more to the point, the feeling of being stared at would stop. So you're gay. Plenty of people are gay. Get over yourself.

When they talked about this issue—and Sophie brought it up fairly regularly, though that was because she thought Ethan was lonely, and not necessarily because she wanted to win the argument—he mainly listened. He didn't fight back, didn't give reasons, didn't argue his case—which, deep down, infuriated Sophie, although she was very good at exuding a sense of calm. She just didn't understand, and she wanted her friend to explain, but Ethan would tell her that she was one of a handful of people that knew his secret, so she should be happy with that and leave it alone.

The truth was, he didn't know why he wasn't open about his sexuality. He'd had two relationships in his life, both when he was in his early twenties, both short in duration and scant in meaning, and then he had shut down that part of his heart and mind.

Ethan guessed that there were probably hundreds, thousands of people like him—men and women who were unable to talk about who they were, who felt the need to hide a fundamental part of their lives because they were ashamed, unhappy, scared, or confused. He thought he did not open up about his sexuality for the same reason that he did not talk about other areas of his life to individuals he didn't know—or rather, did not allow himself to know. It wasn't that he was ashamed of being gay; it was that being gay was personal, and he didn't like to share personal matters with anyone. Might that characteristic have been different if he had been attracted to the hot young female cheerleader when he was at school instead of the hot young male cheerleader—or if he had fallen for the woman serving coffee in the local Starbucks rather than the man? Maybe; but would he have spoken to either of them anyway? No.

But if Ethan had revealed that part of his argument, he knew, Sophie would have pounced. She would have said, *Yes, if you were a heterosexual you would have spoken to the cheerleader, or, if not the cheerleader, perhaps a less obvious version of that woman, someone you would want to be with. It was because you were a homosexual that you had a myriad of hang-ups and that kept you quiet.* And he would have said *No*, he would not have spoken to the cheerleader or her less showy friends, because the inclination not to speak to *anyone*, let alone objects of his affection, was as much a part of his personality as homosexuality was. He would then have argued that there were probably hundreds of straight guys and girls out there who were alone, who had not acted upon impulse, and who would always be alone because they were scared, confused, or unhappy. Homosexuality, heterosexuality; insecurity was the issue.

Cancer did change the equation, though; he had to admit that. Cancer was threatening his life, and as with many other people who were survivors, cancer was making Ethan examine his life. He was who he was, but was that a good thing? Was he truly happy? And if not, why couldn't he change—especially now, when changing might help him save his life?

This was the question that had started off as a drop of sweet honey on his tongue and soon became a full-blown sugar rush consuming his body and mind. He had asked himself: why would admitting he was gay help save his life? And the answer had been immediate and interesting and exciting. He had forgotten what excitement felt like. He thought, if he did it, it would be a bold and brazen psychological move—and if he'd learned anything over the last few months, it was that cancer was as much a part of a survivor's psychological makeup as it was their physical makeup. Ethan was trying to fight cancer physically through exercise, so why not psychologically? Bold and brazen sounded good as he contemplated a scan that might dictate whether he lived or died.

But if he was going to be bold and brazen, if he was going to "out" himself after many years of secrecy, why would he not make it a really bold and brazen "out"? If he was going to fundamentally change who he was, why not make the change in such an outrageous way as to make it really worth it?

Ethan had always been a student of fate. From his very early years, he had pondered why things happened. In sports, of course, he wanted to know the "what ifs" of the game, but this applied to other areas of life, too. Why had he been born in Detroit, a city with so many flaws—but also so many strengths, so much character? Why did he have a father who had been an uncaring brute? Why did he end up standing across from Sophie in Nemo's, and from where had come that rare spark of verbosity and sense of worthiness that had allowed him to speak to her in a meaningful way?

And fate's long and winding road went on from there. Why had they become best friends? Why, when he had moved down to Florida, did she happen to find a job just after he had moved, a job in the very same area of the state? Why was he diagnosed with cancer, and why did he happen to have a best friend who was an expert in the field of cancer and exercise?

Ethan stood once more and paced as he saw a finish line ahead for his trail of thoughts. Wasn't it strange that Lance Armstrong, whom he idolized, had founded the organization that funded the LIVE**STRONG** at the YMCA program, for which Sophie was a national leader? And wasn't Sophie going down to a conference in Austin soon? Could he out himself in the heart of the LIVE**STRONG** Foundation?

14

~

Every cancer survivor has a memory of the moment when he or she hears the word. When cancer is mentioned, adrenaline flows, hearts beat faster, tears are shed, deep breaths taken. Ethan already knew he was a cancer survivor, but understanding how much of his journey lay ahead, and how little lay behind—that revelation was hard to hear.

His tests were positive, which meant his operation had not caught all of the disease. The doctor let him look at the scan results, and there were a number of spots on his lungs showing that it had metastasized and was now possibly working its way around his body.

He had been stunned, and he realized that even though he had feared a bad result, he had not been expecting one. He listened in silence as his doctor told him that he would be increasing the levels of his medication. He thought a heavier dose of chemo might be Ethan's best hope, that maybe his original tests had not picked up the extent of the disease, and so it was important to give the chemotherapy time to begin working. There was nothing more that could be done except wait and then test again. He had driven away from the doctor's office in a fog of uncertainty, meandered around back streets before eventually reaching home to get his dog so they could head to the most peaceful spot he knew.

His thoughts were more contemplative than he expected, involving more of a sense of overall disappointment than focused distress; but still, he had started to cry at the beach. Almost immediately, Jay left his friends, left his beloved sea, and came to rest his head on Ethan's knees.

How did they do that? What sensory equipment did dogs have aside from a great sense of smell, hearing, and eyesight? Something else hovered around their heads, like emotional radar, or a sensor for distress. Studies showed that dogs could detect sickness in many forms, including epileptic attacks and cancer. Whether it was sadness or illness that was detectable, Jay was there for his master, with a soft head for support.

The tears, however, were not as bad as they might have been, in the same way that Ethan's situation did not feel as bad as it should have felt. He had received the worst news possible, but it had been preceded by a eureka moment, and for as long as he could, he was going to focus on the eureka moment. He planned to call Sophie as soon as possible to tell her his news, and to thank her—she had started a sequence of realizations, and the doctor's news was just a sentence in the paragraph of the last few hours. The tears were certainly tears of sadness, but also relief: at long last, Ethan was determined to inject some honesty and effort into his life.

From his iPad he sent a letter to his boss at Raymond James. He apologized for the form of communication he was using, but explained the situation, let him know about the test results, and told him that he promised to visit within the next few weeks. He ended with a request for more extended time off, so that he could concentrate on the cancer and his recovery.

Ethan then did a search for Tony Cannavaro, Fat-Fingered Tony, and found a few stories about him, including one that listed his accomplishments working for the Associated Press in New York. He found his contact details on their website and sent an e-mail straight away, apologizing for getting in touch out of the blue, describing his situation, and then asking for help.

Just as he was packing up to leave the beach, to make his way back home to try to eat something, he got a response from Raymond James. His boss told him that he was sorry for the diagnosis, that he should take all the time he needed, and that yes, he should come in to Raymond James because they would like to see how else they could be supportive. Once in the car, Ethan dialed Sophie's number.

15

$\sim$

The LIVE**STRONG** at the YMCA program that Ethan was a part of met on Tuesdays and Thursdays, but even though it was a Wednesday, the day after his doctor's visit, he went to the Y anyway. Most of his group came in to do something on the off days, and he saw a number of them talking and waiting around the membership desk. The first thing he did when he arrived was go to Sophie's office, knock, ignore the fact that she was meeting with someone, and go behind her desk to give her a hug. She promised to meet him for lunch, and had a sweet smile on her face when he left to work out.

Ethan intended to go into the wellness center to sit on a bike, to try to continue the process of increasing his stamina levels—but then he noticed a line of yellow shirts heading toward the group exercise room. It turned out that Jenny had decided she would hold a cancer-survivor-only group class, to see if it was of interest to anyone. It was something she had learned from the staff at other Ys around the country, a way to give survivors a different, fun opportunity to move and get their heart rates up, but also to get them used to trying other disciplines and other areas of the Y.

The whole concept of a class setting for exercise was new to Ethan, but it was fun, a mixture of light weights and music designed to interest and challenge everyone. Jenny and Sophie had invited graduates from previous LIVE**STRONG** at the YMCA sessions to join the newest group, so there were about twenty participants in the room. Chairs were set up so that individuals could feel comfortable stopping during the class to rest, and he did not feel in any way shy or ashamed to be the first one forced to sit. Ethan's medication doses had been increased immediately after his latest scan, and he felt tired even when he wasn't moving and trying to keep in step with an enthusiastic instructor and some very rhythmic music. Others took their turns on the chairs at regular intervals, including Dave, who had a bad case of man-rhythm too, and his son Josh, who was in bad physical shape, still dealing with liver cancer. He sat for most of the time.

Those who did other classes as part of their routine thought the survivor-only idea was great. There was an element of pressure in the regularly scheduled, fast-paced, high-energy classes like Power Flex and Body Pump—pressure to keep going, to push harder. Sometimes the anxiety was subconscious, because this was a Y and people at all levels of ability should be able to participate in all levels of classes. But subconscious or not, it was still good to have music and fun moves without too much expectation, specifically for those suffering from cancer.

The group sat together after class, before Ethan met for lunch with Sophie. They talked about how they were, what they were facing, and how their respective cancer journeys were going. Everyone present welcomed him with a hug or a handshake. It seemed as though word had spread about the problems and tests he was having, and so all in the group were appreciative of him being there.

Ethan tried hard to listen and remember details as the circle of individuals shared their experiences. Suzanne was having a down day because it was treatment time and she always felt tired and blue for a few days after she had chemotherapy. It was as much the medication itself as it was mental fatigue: she was on a lifetime maintenance program and so was constantly receiving treatment, and would feel this way at regular intervals for the rest of her life.

Brenda had recently spent the day at the beach with her family, some from Florida and others from out of state. She said it felt really good to be in a normal setting, doing normal family things for the first time in many months.

Everyone seemed to be improving day by day, especially Dave, who had been given a new lease on life because of his involvement in LIVE**STRONG** at the YMCA. He gave a bashful smile as he said that he thought he looked great and had lost a lot of weight. As he spoke, he glanced at his wife every few minutes, a look of adoration on his face. He held her hand on one side, and his son's on the other. All could see that, even as he talked, he was constantly squeezing and stroking Josh's fingers to give him strength.

Josh took his turn speaking and thanked everyone for allowing him to visit and for taking such good care of his dad. He was clearly exhausted and ill, with skin that was taut and yellowing slightly on his face. But the fact that he had come at all clearly gave hope to his parents, and Dave was beaming as his child talked.

When it came to Ethan's turn, he took a deep breath and told them about his test results and the new levels of medication. The great thing about being in a room full of people suffering from cancer was that there were no hysterics, no tears—just looks of understanding and support. All present had been through similar situations, had been given bad news, and had made various decisions on how they were going to make it through. Ethan was asked who his doctor was and about the type of tablet he was taking, how it was affecting him, and if there was anything he needed. It was refreshing to be able to reveal what he was going through and receive only words of support and encouragement in return.

He had lunch with Sophie at the Thirsty Marlin, a short drive from the Y. It was a particularly Floridian local watering hole with indoor and outdoor tables, good fish, good beer, and friendly local staff. Ethan felt better for the exercise, and they sat outside, enjoying a slight breeze and warm sunshine. He tried a grouper sandwich and drank plenty of water, but just picked the fish apart and left the bread. Still, he wasn't there for the food, just the fellowship, so it was a successful lunch. Apologies were offered and refused at the start of the meal—both felt their last conversation had been too edgy—and then two old friends settled back into being best friends.

Sophie wanted to know the results of the tests immediately, and he told her in a matter-of-fact way that seemed to soften the blow, though she shed a few tears and took a moment to absorb the news. They talked a little about the doctor's thoughts on the scan, Ethan's feelings and how he intended to move forward, her thoughts based on knowledge she had from working with oncologists and many, many survivors who had been through her program in different stages of treatment and recovery. She said she thought it had meant a lot to his fellow survivors to see him at such a crucial stage in his treatment, and Ethan told her that the support had felt good. Then he had his own questions to ask.

"Sophie, I want to thank you for being honest with me the other day. It caused me to have a real introspective heart-to-heart with myself. Would you mind if I told you a few things about my younger days, gave you a little more depth on my life?"

"Of course. I'd love to hear more." Sophie's smile was encouraging and her face open and honest.

Ethan talked about his self-analysis, and she nodded along thoughtfully as he revealed more to her about his parents than he ever had before—their marital problems, the violence in the household, attitudes that they held that made them resent the city they lived in even as their son grew to love Detroit. He talked to her about long periods of loneliness that had ended when he met her, and she cried again when he thanked her for being the one person with whom he could be and feel honest.

They sat in silence for a little while, enjoying the breeze and the ocean smells that wafted around the small downtown area of Palm Harbor, before Ethan spoke again.

"Sophie, why are you friends with me?"

Sophie launched into a list of all the good qualities Ethan had as a person, clearly looking to bolster his spirits and ego, so he held up his hand and asked the question again in a different way.

"Why are we so close? Why are we such good friends? What if we hadn't seen each other on some random night in Nemo's?"

She was quiet for a few minutes, and then replied in a more thoughtful way. "Ethan, you have an interesting mix of qualities in your personality. In my opinion, you have many good masculine traits and many good feminine traits, and I don't mean because you are gay. I don't think that has anything to do with it. I think your character—your shyness, your thoughtfulness, and your artistic and literary nature—has mixed with your upbringing and some of the challenges you have faced to create a unique person, and that person has been the perfect foil to the men I have stumbled upon and with whom I've developed relationships."

She took a drink and smiled. "You always talk about how good a friend I've been to you. Well, when things aren't going well for me, with my work or my partner, there are times when I get everything I need out of a man from you, without any of the negative hang-ups. There are also times when you give me everything I need from a friend, even more than I get from my female friends, especially your ability to listen and not talk. So do I often thank God that we met that night in Detroit? Heavens, yes!"

Now there were tears in Ethan's eyes, and he leaned over and gave Sophie a gentle kiss on the forehead before taking a deep breath so that he could ask her for help once again.

"Sophie, you have convinced me that being honest with myself and others should go hand in hand with my struggle with cancer. The more I think about it, the more I believe that this disease is a small twist of fate like many others that have occurred in my life.

"I feel really strongly that I want to continue to follow this path of fortune because it will help me open up as a person and open up as a survivor. The trail I see in my mind leads from Detroit to Clearwater to Austin."

The look on his friend's face was a mixture of happiness and interest, so he forged on. "When I think about you, I get an enormous rush of emotion, because you've been my friend for so long. But now, because of cancer, some of that emotion is also tied to the LIVE**STRONG** Foundation, because of what the organization means to you and because of the help I've received through you and through them. Sophie, could I come to Austin with you, to the home of the foundation? Could you make this happen?"

Part Two

~

A Love Letter

To Whom It May Concern:

I would like to thank the YMCA for welcoming me to the *LIVE***STRONG** at the YMCA program. You have fantastic instructors, in particular Maureen. Everyone is patient, with gentle but firm guidance, and as a group, we feel comfortable sharing humor and sadness while working out.

Our program has many people with "special" needs, and the Y staff show great flexibility in dealing with each individual. Thanks to the *LIVE***STRONG** at the YMCA program I have begun to rebuild muscle and body strength which had been decimated by stage four ovarian cancer and two major surgeries, a colostomy and six chemo treatments in three months. I was so frail I feared walking at malls, on sidewalks or trying to exercise at home. I am now working full time and have the confidence to get back out there to have fun and enjoy my life.

Thank you for all of your help.
LIVE**STRONG** at the YMCA participant, 2010

February 2012

16

E than always believed his friend when she said that LIVE**STRONG** at the YMCA was lifesaving, but *hearing* and believing and *experiencing* and believing were two different things.

He delved a little deeper into the science of the program on test day, when his fitness levels as a cancer survivor returning to exercise were assessed. At the end of twelve weeks, a second assessment would be made and statistics gathered, to encourage him, but also to provide data that would justify this work to senior staff, board members, and donors.

Normally Ethan would have had this assessment right at the start of the program with his group, but because he'd had some unique struggles, Sophie and Jenny made the decision to test him on his own. He had also been exercising for a while, unlike the others, who had been assessed before being introduced to the wellness center—but again, the staff made a special case for him because they felt he needed a baseline to see improvement.

Ethan had been nervous, thinking about how debilitated he was from his treatments, so to set his mind at ease and to help him get prepared, Sophie had given him the guidelines that all of the instructors used, outlining the tests and the step-by-step approach they used. The document was the same for all staff around the country, and showed how much thought had gone into the program and its standardization. It also made

Ethan feel better, thinking about survivors all around America who were doing what he was doing.

The tests they did to assess his aerobic function were a six-minute walk test, a one-repetition maximum on the leg press, and a one-repetition maximum on the chest press. For flexibility they did a back-scratch test, an arm-reach test, and a single-leg balance test.

Ethan felt like he was back at school as he tried each exercise and Jenny scribbled scores on a pad. Physically, it was clear that he was weak, but maybe not as weak as he had expected to be. On the six-minute walk test he was fine; on the leg press one-repetition max he aimed way too high with the weight and had to drop to a more realistic level, and even that caused him to stress and strain as he completed the rep. But he completed it. The same thing happened with the chest press, and Jenny had to lean over and give him just a little help to complete the lift.

The areas where Ethan struggled most involved flexibility and balance. The back-scratch test felt like torture. Reaching both arms behind his back to try to touch fingertips made him feel like he was on an old medieval rack. His struggles were undoubtedly as much a reflection of his long-term general inactivity levels as they were his problems with cancer. He was just not supple. Same with the arm reach, and then, when it came to the balance test, he was totally frustrated at his inability to stand on one leg.

Jenny ruffled Ethan's hair when he was done. "You know, everyone is disappointed in some way when they finish the initial assessment. Then again, most participants are excited and proud when they get their post-assessment results and see how much they have progressed. I think you're going to improve a lot in the next several weeks, but I think you did well on the strength and endurance sections here."

"I understand weakness and lack of endurance," Ethan replied, "but I've fallen over twice in my house in the last couple of days, and so my balance issues are a big concern."

"I think you should keep investigating the type of cancer you have and also look at the LIVE**STRONG** Foundation website. It has a lot of information that might help you understand what you're going through. Knowledge is power, Ethan, remember."

Jenny took him over to a resource table that had been set up for survivors in the lobby, and after browsing through leaflets and pamphlets for a few minutes, they found just the thing. Their success underscored the breadth of the LIVE**STRONG** at the YMCA program and the LIVE**STRONG** Foundation. The programs weren't just about helping people to exercise, but also about providing them with resources and information.

BALANCE AND MOBILITY

What helps us to keep our balance and mobility? The body's nerves and muscles are highly involved in maintaining balance and mobility. Balance is the ability to keep us stable, on our feet, and able to perform certain activities. Balance also prevents us from falling down from a standing or sitting position. Mobility allows us to move around and react to our environment in a timely manner. There are certain areas of the body that help us to keep our balance. One of these areas is the cerebellum, which is located behind the brain stem and controls functions of movement, balance, mobility, and posture. If you have experienced damage to your cerebellum, you will experience impaired mobility, imbalance, and incoordination. The vestibular system of the inner ear also plays an important role in helping to maintain our balance. It sends and interprets signals from the environment to keep us erect, and the body in balance when we move.

What are the causes of imbalance? Many medications, treatments, and diseases can affect these areas, commonly causing problems with imbalance, dizziness, and our mobility, in general. Examples of conditions or medications that may affect the cerebellum or vestibular system include many chemotherapy drugs. These drugs may also affect the vestibular system of the inner ear.

Individuals should also be aware of the effects of dehydration on balance. If you are dehydrated, and you change positions, you may experience dizziness. This is a result of low blood pressure (orthostatic hypotension). Your healthcare provider may check your vital signs (including your blood pressure and heart rate) while lying down, sitting up, and standing, to help in determining this. Weakness caused by stress, fever, fatigue, anemia, heart problems, or stroke may also cause dizziness and imbalance.

Infection or inflammation of the inner ear, brain, or spinal cord may cause unsteadiness and you may notice imbalance after prolonged bed rest, when your muscles weaken. This will also lead to problems with general mobility.

Sophie found Ethan reading the leaflet and, when she heard about the problems he was having, said that if she were a gambler, she would bet on medication being the culprit. She then smiled, slapped her own wrist, and told him to see his doctor.

She was very excited that he had completed his assessment and thought his scores were good; certainly on par with others and excellent considering everything that he had been through. She asked a few more questions about the tests and then focused on his efforts to learn more about the fellow cancer survivors in his group.

Sophie encouraged, maybe even demanded, that Ethan do this—to help force himself out of the self-imposed shell he had crawled into, but also to help other participants who were going through their own challenges. She also expected his cooperation because she had stuck to her part of the agreement and had registered her friend for the LIVE**STRONG** Assembly. He was responsible for his expenses, flight, and accommodations, but since every Y was only supposed to be bringing one representative, Sophie had pulled some strings to make sure Ethan could attend as a volunteer and cancer survivor involved in the program itself.

The assembly was a gathering of all of the foundation's partners, not just the YMCA. Any organization, large or small, funded by the foundation to help cancer survivors in their own communities had been invited to send a representative. The hope was that they could network, brainstorm, and gather ideas to further their own efforts. Also, if they could build relationships with potential partners who were also present in their home city or state, these partners might be able to provide additional support and resources.

Sophie had emphasized that her friend's attendance at the assembly was dependent on him fulfilling the other parts of the agreement. What was important, to Sophie at least, was his commitment to help and engage with the group. She really felt like the support and camaraderie that was generated by involvement in the LIVE**STRONG** at the YMCA program was in many ways as important as the benefits that came from physical exercise.

On an inner level, Ethan knew that he was beginning to experience those benefits, the results of working out, even though he had been hard on himself following the assessment. With the encouragement of Jenny, Sophie, and other survivors, he could now ride the bike longer without stopping and had begun to strengthen his muscles with a basic routine involving free weights and machines. He had started regularly pairing up with Dave and Steve so that they could support and cajole each other as they did their sets: arm curls, shoulder presses, and bench presses, with very limited weight for Ethan compared to his two stronger friends, of course—but nevertheless, with weight.

Dave was an inspiration, and he had a heart-wrenching story. He was and always had been overweight, sometimes chronically so; and this had led to heart problems, diabetes, and depression caused by living with those conditions. On top of these issues, he had been diagnosed with cancer of the spleen at the same time that his son had begun treatment for liver cancer. This had plunged him deeper into depression. It was his wife Mary and her constant nagging that had driven him to the Y and the LIVE**STRONG** at the YMCA program.

The gradual implementation of an exercise regimen had begun to have a real effect on all of Dave's ailments, not just his recovery from cancer. This was actually his second time through LIVE**STRONG** at the YMCA, which didn't happen often—but the structured nature of the session and the support that was an intrinsic part of each group had helped him so much that Sophie had made the decision to allow him back in for one more go-round.

Mary cried whenever she talked about the progress he had made, and the fact that his sunny disposition had reappeared because he felt like he had been given a second chance. This was something he really appreciated. She left him alone when he was in the Y with his group, but they often exercised together on alternate days, and their joy as they helped and encouraged each other was palpable for all in the wellness center to share.

Dave was a bear of a man and could lift three times what Ethan could, but he, too, had been in Ethan's place—weak and fatigued—and so he was good at cajoling and guiding him in just the right way.

The same was true of Steve. He was out of treatment, but even though he had always been fit and strong, he could remember struggling with lethargy and that feeling of frailty that caused a unique level of anxiety in an athlete. Now he was in relatively good shape—great shape, compared to the rest of the program's participants—and back doing full-time work as an athletic director at Tarpon Springs High School. For him, LIVE**STRONG** at the YMCA was about education and support and he made it clear often that he was finding these ingredients in abundance.

After exercise, the entire group would sit in the lobby and talk, drink coffee, and revel in their accomplishments. Ethan knew he had to make an effort to mingle, and so on one particular day, he grabbed a chair next to Suzanne, a striking lady perhaps in her mid-fifties and sporting long, silver hair.

He asked her if she would share more about what she had been through, and she smiled and said, "Of course!" Like many of the survivors, she was happy to talk, because she thought the verbalization of her experiences was personally therapeutic, and because she understood that it was often beneficial for others.

"Well, Ethan, five years ago I was diagnosed with multiple myeloma, which is an incurable blood cancer. I went through several treatments, including chemotherapy and a stem-cell transplant, but the results were mixed. I am in remission, but I'll need treatment for life."

Suzanne not only shared her story, but her strength also when she spoke. It resonated in her voice and shone from her eyes. She was very inspiring. "Initially, I suffered from such debilitating fatigue, and after a relapse and more chemotherapy, the one constant continued to be fatigue. I was exhausted, always—when I was working, playing, eating. When I first came to the LIVE**STRONG** at the YMCA program, I had such a profound lack of confidence in myself. I didn't think I had the ability to do what was necessary to be stronger. And then, of course, Jenny and Sophie stepped in."

Suzie, as she wanted to be called, seemed to enjoy telling her story, but then wanted to know about Ethan. She was a very good listener, and he made a mental note to tell Sophie that she had a survivor in her group with exemplary "listen first" skills. Suzie listened and asked a lot of open-ended questions that Ethan knew were designed to encourage him to talk more, to open up in different ways on different topics.

The technique worked. It felt good for him to share with someone other than Sophie—and the great thing was, there were similarities in some of their experiences. She was able to offer some thoughts and interesting ideas that Ethan was going to try, to help him work through the treatment phase of his disease.

One thing Suzie did that surprised him at first was reach up and, without preamble, pull off her hair—which turned out to be a silver wig. She proudly displayed her smooth, bald head, and everyone around her laughed aloud at her obvious theatrics. When she heard the laughter, she stood and took a bow, then nonchalantly placed the wig back on her head and asked Ethan to straighten it until he thought it looked good.

Her performance was in response to his comments about hair loss, and the fact that since the increase in the potency of his oral chemotherapy, he'd been depressed to find clumps of hair on his pillow each morning or on the bathroom floor after he took a shower. She revealed that she had shaved her head pretty quickly after her diagnosis, and now kept it shaved because of the constant treatment she was still receiving, which made her natural hair thin and unattractive.

The relaxed way in which Suzie unveiled her baldness, showing the whole lobby that she had no hair, was very reassuring. If this beautiful middle-aged lady, who had perhaps been more conscious of her looks and the need to maintain a look because of her position as a woman in a superficial world, could shave her head, then Ethan decided straight away that he needed to do the same.

17

Ethan rarely talked about his sexuality, even to Sophie. In the early stages of their friendship, when cordial had changed to close, she had probed a little and heard the tale of his two collegiate flings, neither initiated by him and neither long-lasting. When he spoke about that period in his life, Ethan wrinkled his nose, and the names Karl and Richard rolled off his tongue like stale air, leaving a bad taste in his mouth. After that one revelation, he placed the topic off-limits, using humor or honest avoidance to move on to more desirable conversational grounds.

So Sophie realized the risk she was taking when she decided to lean a little harder on her friend—but it had worked out. She could not believe the transformation, and also could not believe that a plan, hastily formulated in her head, had worked so well. She had wanted to push Ethan, which was not necessarily her role as a YMCA coach, but perhaps was her role as a friend. She had wanted to push him out into the middle of his cancer survivor cadre, so that they could guide, teach, and inspire him, and so that he could reciprocate with new friends. She had also tried to use this psychological shove to affect other areas of his life, to achieve a long-term goal, had wanted to help her friend open up in so many ways, and to a degree—perhaps internally more than externally at the moment—it seemed to have worked.

Many of the survivors in the LIVE**STRONG** at the YMCA group had asked her about the very sudden transformation in her friend. They talked about how much his demeanor had changed, how his approach to the program had changed, and how he had revealed more in a few days than he had in weeks before. Ethan had even thanked her.

Of course there was a road still to walk—many roads still to walk on a cancer journey that would inevitably affect the life journey. But Sophie had more confidence now that her friend might be able to gather some tools around him to help him fight.

The question about the LIVESTRONG assembly had taken her completely by surprise and was not an outcome she had expected. However, the thought process that Ethan had followed was logical, and even ingenious.

"If I'm going to out myself, Sophie—and you do want me to out myself—why would I not do it in the most meaningful location imaginable?"

She had no idea what that might look like and had no idea what trouble she might be getting herself into, but really, she had no choice. Ethan had embraced her challenge and had set one in return.

What had been impressive was her conversation with the LIVESTRONG Foundation staff. She had debated whether to make something up, but then recited the YMCA mission and values to herself and simply called a colleague at the foundation and laid the scenario at her feet.

"Well, Sophie, I have heard many stories in my time here, as you can imagine, but that is a unique one. Here's what I think. We're all here to help and support cancer survivors, so if you think attending the assembly will help Ethan, then he should come."

The fact that Sophie's friend could even come to an invitation-only event that was packed, and the ease with which he had been allowed to come, impressed her, though she shouldn't have been surprised. She, of all people, knew how committed the LIVESTRONG Foundation was to survivors, and how supportive it was of the YMCA and its members.

She just hoped all of this worked out the way Ethan wanted it to. Her friend had tossed all his cards in one pile and that pile was fate, so, it seemed, what would be would be. The next few weeks would be exciting, frightening, inspiring, but for Sophie, that was often the case anyway. That was why she loved her job.

18

It felt like, in the blink of an eye, with one action, Ethan was able to make giant strides in his search for personal liberation and freedom from disease. One moment he was sitting shaggy and tired in front of a bathroom mirror with Sophie hovering nervously over him, electric clippers humming; and the next, he was bald-headed and relaxed with Sophie now smiling, clippers silent, wet razor coated in soap and hair in her hand. His friend had been surprised when he had called her and asked her to come to his house to shave his head. Then he told her about Suzie and her performance in the lobby, and her perfect listen-first skills, and she understood. She knew Suzie well.

There was a DVD that was provided to each YMCA that began a cancer survivor program for the first time, a DVD called *LIVESTRONG Manifesto*. Sophie had shown it to Ethan a couple of times, when she had first gotten involved in the program and when her friend had first been diagnosed with cancer. It was a powerful visual and audio statement in pictures and words, detailing the LIVE**STRONG** Foundation's reason for being. One series of video clips showed cancer survivors in various stages of their fight against the disease, and one scene showed a husband leaving his bedroom to shave his head in support of his wife, who was undergoing treatment and was bald. Ethan reminded Sophie of that piece before she began in her role as his barber.

It was tough, but not so tough, because he had a friend and supporter to help. Despite his age, Ethan did not have a bad head of hair, and there was a twinge of anxiety when his bare skin began to show. He could only imagine what the feeling might be like for women. Men, at least, constantly faced the threat of baldness, whereas for women hair was a statement of femininity.

There was sensuality in Sophie's work. She cut a tramline along her friend's head, then stroked the bristles before moving on to another section and stroking again. Soaping and shaving was easy, and ten minutes after the first cut, Sophie kissed a smooth head and it was done. Ethan stood and turned; there was a nervous moment, and then they stood arm in arm in front of the mirror and laughed.

They stayed that way for a few minutes as Ethan pointed to various scars revealed by the haircut and told the stories behind them, and then they walked from the bathroom into the living room, turned the TV to a news channel, and lay on the couch, listening and occasionally commenting on the events that were happening around the nation and the world.

Sophie left while Ethan was still wide awake, which was unusual. When she visited, he normally fell asleep on the couch or in a chair, and she would either leave or guide him to his room before letting herself out the front door. A few times since the treatment began, Sophie had stayed the night. Ethan often found it hard to sleep continuously through the night, even though he was exhausted. He felt sick and needed to stagger to the bathroom, or, more often than not, he just he woke up with a head full of thoughts. When this happened, he would have to get up and do something to take his mind off of cancer and the consequences of cancer before he could get back to sleep again.

When Ethan told his friend about the issues he had at night, she was immediately concerned and wanted to help—but in his eyes, she was already doing more than enough, and she had her own life to live. Regardless, oblivious to all objections, when he was feeling particularly under the weather, Sophie camped in the spare room in case she was needed.

Sometimes Ethan's thoughts at night were philosophical and focused on survivorship as a whole. He pondered the overall cancer experience and wondered what it would be like without even a basic support system in place. He would think of Dave and his wife, and Suzie and her husband, who didn't exercise with her, but came to pick her up often and stayed to chat with her YMCA friends. He tried to imagine how he would be without Sophie. He wondered how he would be without an understanding employer who had allowed him to go home and recover with no questions, no cut in pay or benefits. He knew that did not happen often.

He wondered what it was like for survivors who did not have LIVE**STRONG** at the YMCA, a program that was so important to Sophie in her career and in her need for a mission focus, a program that had quickly become a focal point for Ethan, too, Mr. Health Seeker finding gratification in just riding a little more and bench-pressing a little more. What would it be like for all his new teammates, his new friends, if they didn't have hope provided by an opportunity to urge and work their bodies and minds back to health? What would it be like to be a lonely cancer survivor?

Unfortunately, there had to be hundreds, if not thousands, out there who were just that: lonely and sick. When Ethan had these thoughts, he realized even more clearly how important a charity like the LIVE**STRONG** Foundation was—an organization focused solely on providing support and resources to cancer survivors in so many ways.

Ethan had finally received a kind and encouraging e-mail back from his former editor, Tony. Yes, he remembered him from their Detroit days; he was sad and sorry to hear about his illness, and happy to help in any way he could. He described how he had left Detroit because he wanted a change of scenery, and wanted to expand his horizons when it came to news reporting. The Associated Press had given him the perfect opportunity to do that, especially since it served over 1,700 newspapers around the country and had over 300 locations worldwide.

Tony had asked some professional questions about involvement in journalism, reporting, or writing, but had also peppered his correspondence with personal touches. The e-mail, in general, reminded Ethan of his former colleague: it was thoughtful and inquisitive, even sensitive, and that belied the visual image of Fat-Fingered Tony. When Ethan had first heard that nickname, after a couple of weeks as an intern at the *Free Press*, he had cringed. It seemed cruel, a dig at the man's weight and Italian heritage, which in part meant his love of Italian cooking—but actually, there was more to the story.

An assistant editor who had worked with Tony for several years told Ethan that the nickname was really an affectionate celebration of his early years as a reporter covering crime in Detroit. Tony had been very successful at investigating and writing stories on crime families in the area, particularly the Detroit Partnership, one of the most infamous Mafia families outside of New York. He'd also written a series of articles on the connection between Jimmy Hoffa of the teamsters and the Mafia, and was rumored to be friends with Joe Zerilli, the highest-ranking family member in Detroit. If that weren't enough, he also knew one of Zerilli's closest associates, Michael Santo Polizzi, "Big Mike."

It was Zerilli who was supposed to have famously taken the knowledge of the whereabouts of Jimmy Hoffa's body to his grave, but it was Tony's association with Big Mike that earned him his nickname. His colleagues at the time had agreed that he had to have a nickname, considering the people with whom he associated—and the one image of Tony that everyone agreed was iconic, amazing to watch, was the image of him crouched over a typewriter or keyboard, big fingers flying furiously from letter to letter as he produced amazing story after amazing story. And so, "Fat-Fingered Tony" was born.

To have Tony Cannavaro encourage Ethan to write was so meaningful, and Tony's words made him stop and think again. It was hard to imagine how he could change any more, after his cancer diagnosis and his decision to begin to acknowledge his sexuality. But Tony's feedback made him shake his head and wonder exactly what he had been doing for the past twenty-two or so years, working as an accountant. He had pursued this career almost indifferently, because he was good at it and because it would clearly make him money, and his family needed money. If he was honest with himself, it was also an easy path to take, and in his past and since, he had leaned too often toward easy.

A few weeks ago, this e-mail and these thoughts might have engulfed

Ethan with sorrow, might have caused him to be riddled with regret alongside his cancer—but it was time to move on. Tony had signed off by recommending a book written by a young cancer survivor, Marc Woods, a Brit who had lost his leg at a young age but went on to swim for his country, winning numerous medals in the Paralympics. Tony said it had been inspirational to him and might, perhaps, be a tale that would help bring meaning to Ethan's own story, the one he was living. Ethan bought the book online for his iPad, and the introduction alone had an immediate effect.

My life might have been so different.

Have you seen the film *Sliding Doors*? It's a film that explores one of those big questions in life: what if? In the film we see "what is" and "what might have been." The main character is sacked from work and sets off for home via the London Underground: in one version of her life she catches a Tube train; in another version, she misses it. An arbitrary event—the time she arrives at the train platform—sends her life in two totally different directions, and the audience gets to see how both versions play out.

Countless events shape the course of our lives, some significantly, some less so. And, as we get older, who doesn't look back on life and reflect on how things might have been? What would my life have been like if I'd passed that exam? If I'd not lost that job? If I hadn't met the person I married?

The question I always come back to is: what would my life have been like if I hadn't got cancer? I think I know the answer.

In my life without cancer, I make the passage from teenager to adult like any ordinary teenager, untroubled by responsibility, unburdened by cares. Average at school, I remain average at college; I get an average job and I tick along, making do, getting by. I get a family, a house, and a mortgage.

The one escape in my life is swimming. I was a good swimmer as a boy and I remain a good swimmer. A county level swimmer—but never an *excellent* swimmer. Because that kind of excellence requires the kind of commitment that an average person just doesn't have. Not me, anyway. So, all in all, ordinary person, ordinary life.

Like *Sliding Doors*, the "what is" version of my life is in stark contrast to the "what might have been" version. Not for me the carefree years of teenage irresponsibility. Oh no. In this one I'm minding my own business when I get a swollen ankle. "So what?" you say. Well, somehow, the swollen ankle turns into cancer. Not just any cancer either, but a nasty virulent cancer of the bone. The doctors tell me that if I don't have part of my leg amputated, I'll die. And if I do, I still might die—I'll have a 50-50 chance, instead of no chance. So, minus part of my leg, I endure six courses of chemo and survive.

The one escape in my life is swimming. A good swimmer as a boy, I become an excellent swimmer—a member of the British swimming team and a highly competitive, motivated, committed athlete. My brush with mortality, ironically, makes me realize that I am capable of much more than I ever imagined. I set myself some tough challenges and I achieve them. I knuckle down, strap myself in, and ride life's roller coaster. I win gold, silver, and bronze medals. More than that, I climb mountains, do charitable work—I even write a book. Ordinary person, extraordinary life. Well, halfway there, maybe.

Do I regret the way my life has turned out? No, not for a minute. I'm not going to say cancer is the best thing that ever happened to me. That's too glib, too easy. I wouldn't wish what I've been through on anyone else.

But having cancer has made me a better person. It's taught me to approach life in a different way. It's taught me to measure myself against my potential and not against others'. It has taught me about personal responsibility: that life is about being the best person you can be and a lot more besides.

If you are lucky, life teaches you what you don't learn at school. I've been very lucky. I've learned some tough but invaluable lessons about life on my journey. I'd like to share those lessons with you.

Ethan didn't want to be average at life anymore. He wanted to set himself big goals. He wanted to beat cancer; he wanted to help others beat cancer; he wanted to help his friend as she organized one of the biggest events of her life, the LIVE**STRONG** Assembly—and while helping her, he wanted to meet one of the greatest cancer survivors of all time. At the same time, he wanted to change his career completely. Ethan decided he wanted to write, in some way, some form, because it was what he loved to do—and he wanted to be good at what he loved, not average at what he disliked.

19

Barriers began to fall in front of Ethan with great regularity as he progressed in the LIVE**STRONG** at the YMCA program. When he finally rode an upright bike for the first time since his diagnosis, it felt like crossing a finishing line—though much of the race still lay ahead. An upright bike was more traditional than the recumbent he had been confined to during his time at the Y, and it made sweat stream off his bald head and down his face after only ten minutes of pedaling. His energy levels were still shot, which was frustrating. But he kept going, following the lead of Brenda, a fellow survivor who was funny and feisty and on her own bike next to him. She told the group one day that she had a newly installed willpower generator, which she had nicknamed her "triple P motor." Triple P stood for "Perseverance, Prayer, and Pissedoffedness." When she explained the concept, she even spelled *pissedoffedness* to make sure everyone got it.

Brenda was a spitfire, and her energy motivated the entire group. After spending a little more time with her, Ethan found out she was quite a local celebrity when it came to cancer awareness. She was a volunteer with the local chapter of the American Cancer Society and a member of the Palm Harbor health advisory board, and was most famous for staging a twenty-four-hour sit-in at the local library because they had removed a cancer awareness literature table in favor of a selection of big-budget movies for rent on DVD. Ethan had found an interview she had done for local TV after the sit-in, and he'd watched her destroy the reputation of the library executive director at the time with a mixture of spot-on facts and caustic humor.

The wellness center in the Y had a line of cardio machines that faced a big window so that as a member walked or ran, in the middle of their pleasure or pain, they could look out at cars and people, people arriving to join in with the rituals of health seeking, or leaving sweat-stained and happy because they had done their duty to body and mind. If real life was not a good enough distraction, a line of big-screen televisions mounted near the ceiling were tuned to various sports and news channels. It had just been announced that the government had decided to stop investigating Lance Armstrong, and the press release was headlining as a sports and regular news story.

> United States Attorney André Birotte Jr. today announced that his office is closing an investigation into allegations of federal criminal conduct by members and associates of a professional bicycle racing team owned in part by Lance Armstrong. The United States Attorney determined that a public announcement concerning the closing of the investigation was warranted by numerous reports about the investigation in media outlets around the world.
>
> Mr. Birotte commended the joint investigative efforts of his prosecutors and special agents with the U.S. Food and Drug Administration, the Federal Bureau of Investigation and the United States Postal Service - Office of the Inspector General.

Ethan was biased, of course, but to him, the whole investigation seemed pointless. He happened to believe that Lance was not guilty of doping, and thought that the advantage he gained over his opponents was God-given in the form of a mental toughness built during a terrifying battle against testicular cancer that had spread to the lungs and brain. He also thought Lance had a physical advantage with a body that had rebuilt itself, returned to fitness after being ravaged not only by cancer, but by the drugs designed to destroy cancer, to burn cancer to death.

It was a fact that even before the disease, Lance Armstrong had a body with a freakish VO2 max—the maximum capacity of an individual's body to transport and use oxygen during exercise—and he had demonstrated this with racing potential and wins from an early age. He had been tested for performance-enhancing drugs repeatedly, more so than any other rider as he built up his string of Tour de France wins, and had never failed a test. It didn't seem as though there was any evidence against him, except for the testimonies of former cyclists who had been caught cheating, tested positive, and been thrown out of the sport. They now needed to earn a living—and what better way to do that than to write a book and jump on the gravy train that involved accusing Lance Armstrong?

But whether Lance had cheated or not was not the point—at least not to Ethan. Lance Armstrong's last Tour de France win had been in 2005, and since then, his cancer survivor work had become the focal point of his persona and the main connection with his name. The Lance Armstrong Foundation, which had become known as the LIVE**STRONG** Foundation, was one of the most successful charities helping cancer survivors and certainly one of the most well known. What would be gained by revealing that Lance Armstrong had been a cheat? There was an argument that it would discourage future cheaters, but it seemed as though the cycling world's vigorous anti-doping initiatives were already doing that, with many big-name cyclists being caught. Ethan thought the negative effects on the ability of the foundation to do its work and raise money, along with the negative effects on hundreds of thousands of cancer survivors who looked up to Lance Armstrong as a source of hope and inspiration, would outweigh the positive.

As part of the news story, ESPN showed clips of Lance's greatest rides. Ethan's personal favorite was Armstrong's infamous look back to archrival Jan Ullrich on Alpe d'Huez in 2001. The ease with which he had pulled away up that mountainous incline put into perspective Ethan's efforts on the bike. Just as he was about to stop riding, he thought of Sophie, and he thought of triple P, and he thought of Lance himself, and so he knuckled down for another few minutes.

Those few minutes turned into five as another interesting news story came on, this time involving the debate over same-sex marriage. The screen showed a color-coded map of the country indicating which states had already legalized same-sex marriage, which states had legislation pending, and in which states gay marriage was unlawful. The story was about Washington state, where Governor Chris Gregoire had just signed into law a measure legalizing same-sex marriage—just as one of the Republican presidential hopefuls, Rick Santorum, had arrived in town to campaign. Santorum was against gay marriage, stating that, as opposed to heterosexual marriage, it was of no benefit to society. Therefore, why legalize it?

Pondering the question made Ethan forget the pain of cycling for another couple of minutes, until a throbbing in his quads made him stop. He was wondering: when he eventually completely acknowledged that he was gay and actually wound up getting into a relationship, would he want to get married?

The question was interesting not only because of the gay marriage debate, but because Ethan had not really experienced the benefits of marriage in person. His parents' union had been dysfunctional and abusive, and they had been better off apart than together. Added to that was the fact that his best friend Sophie had suffered through a very unhappy marriage. Would he want to get married if it were legal for a gay person to do so? It was a good question, one he continued to consider as he staggered away from the bike toward the locker room.

20

O ne afternoon at the Y, Ethan and Sophie were talking about the sudden about-face by prosecutors investigating the doping allegations surrounding Lance Armstrong, and discussing how good this was for the LIVE**STRONG** Foundation and for all of their partners involved in helping cancer survivors. The worry and effort that had gone into preparing for the worst had certainly caused resources to be channeled in the wrong direction. There had even been talking points sent around to all YMCAs in case there were questions asked about the Y's involvement with the foundation and the appropriateness of such involvement. For a time, there were concerns about loss of donors, loss of grant opportunities, even loss of community respect.

During this conversation, Ethan happened to mention how much he was looking forward to hearing Lance Armstrong speak in person, and Sophie became fidgety and red. It seemed she was now unsure if Lance would actually be at the assembly. He had a busy schedule and was training for a triathlon, and it was really hard to confirm whether he would be in attendance or not.

They had been chatting in the lobby before a LIVE**STRONG** at the YMCA session, and as Ethan picked up his bag to get changed, he just breathed deeply and shrugged. When Sophie gave him a bemused look, he took a second deep breath and spoke.

"That's a shame, but it's the LIVE**STRONG** Foundation I'm focused on now, not it's founder."

His friend smiled, relieved that Ethan was not more upset by her revelation. "Hey, you'll get four full days of me. What more could you want?"

The conversation lingered in Ethan's mind, and when he got on his bike, he continued to think. What did he expect to gain by going to the assembly? What change did he think would occur? He decided that the answer was the same for him as it was for survivors around the country, around the globe: the LIVE**STRONG** Assembly, and the foundation as a whole, represented hope—hope for strength in the face of adversity, and hope for life after cancer.

Like thousands of others, Ethan hoped for recovery—but he also hoped for the inner strength to discover himself after forty-six years, the strength to look for a normal life—a life free from cancer, but also a life without hidden feelings, a life that contained love. He knew that he had not experienced the variety of love that others had experienced, and that was disappointing. He had loved his parents, his dad for a while, but that had been an example of a love soured, spoiled, and coated with guilt and anger. He had had two brief, experimental relationships that had not contained an ounce of love. And then there was Sophie, whom Ethan loved deeply—but that was friendship love, not partner-for-life love.

A scene from a movie came to mind as he rode his bike. In *Good Will Hunting*, when Robin Williams's character asked Matt Damon's character if he felt like he was alone, Matt Damon replied, "What?" And Robin Williams asked him, "Do you have a soul mate?" Then Matt Damon asked him to define "soul mate," to which Robin Williams replied, "Somebody who challenges you." Matt Damon thought for a minute and then answered, "Chuckie." Robin Williams then said, "No, Chuckie is family. He'd lie down in traffic for you. I'm talking about someone who opens up things for you, touches your soul."

For some reason, he had never felt comfortable enough in himself, in his family, or in his surroundings to begin to talk about and look for someone to love. But now it felt like cancer had stripped everything away.

His best friend was helping him look for a new beginning, and she was using the concept of openness, love, and the LIVE**STRONG** at the YMCA program to do that. There was an intimacy to this process of rebirth that included the strangeness of his connection to Sophie and the hope that came with his new connection to the LIVE**STRONG** Foundation. Ethan could sense instant karma in the distance, and the potential for a metaphysical and physical recovery was breathtaking.

It was interesting how exercise seemed to encourage deep thought—or maybe it was deep thought that helped encourage exercise. Ethan's legs churned away on the bike, albeit slowly, and time flew by. When he woke from his trance, he went and found Dave, and they began to lift free weights instead of using the machines. He only did free weights when he was with Steve or Dave, because they were knowledgeable and good, strong spotters. Ethan had strength issues, but also coordination and balance issues, so he didn't trust himself with an unhinged bar or dumbbell.

As they worked out, he noticed Dave's wife peering through a window from the hallway outside. She really was committed to her husband, and vice versa. When Dave saw her looking in, he waved and happily blew her a kiss, not caring if anyone was watching. They were a couple that was in love and proud of it.

That display of affection took Ethan on a train of thought that ended back with the assembly, and Ethan wondered—if Lance Armstrong was not speaking, then who was? He really hoped Lance was going to be there, began for a few moments to stress about Lance not being there—and then closed his eyes and took a deep breath. He had to practice what he had begun to preach. He had to have faith.

21

Ethan spent most of the next day regretting pushing himself too hard at the Y. After the previous day's workout, he had come home and picked up Jay and driven down to Honeymoon Island for a walk. He had still been thinking about Lance, and then his mind had turned to the news story he had seen about gay marriage. He started pondering what it must mean to get married, thinking about the uproar that the idea of gay marriage was causing, realizing again that it wasn't always easy to be gay—or at least openly gay.

The idea of admitting who he was and what he felt—of coming out—was intimidating; but while he in no way thought that having cancer was a good thing, the disease had undoubtedly given Ethan courage. There was still a stigma attached to cancer—subconscious, perhaps, but a stigma all the same—that manifested itself in surprised or pitying looks, gestures, or comments that slipped out: expressions of alarm at the thought of coming into contact with a frightening disease.

He had seen the signs of that alarm, more so now than ever, on the faces of people on the street, now that he was bald and gaunt. He had seen it, too, occasionally, on the faces of individuals in the wellness center as this group of yellow-shirted individuals exercised together, often laughing their way through strain and gain which nevertheless did not lessen the pity when it appeared. Some, Ethan knew, still saw cancer as a death sentence, and laughter could not trump death. But it was just occasional pity, or sometimes sadness, in the Y. More often than not, there was pleasure, shared laughter, words of kindness and encouragement, and a sense of camaraderie—because whether survivor, health seeker, or very fit person, all present were testing and pushing their bodies to make them stronger and healthier. One of the YMCA's many taglines was that it was open to all, and in Ethan's experience, the Y lived up to that saying.

Maybe an openly gay man would experience similar reactions, just occasional pity or disapproval. Sophie had told Ethan she knew six members of the YMCA who were gay and not afraid to flaunt it, members who came in now and then as partners, who, when alone, talked about their partners, commented on holidays and meals out together, who held hands and gave other public displays of affection to each other. Sophie made the argument that of course there were probably people who frowned upon this, upon homosexuality in general and certainly upon openly displayed homosexuality, but that frowning was not the norm—tolerance was. If he could make it through his cancer, letting everyone know that he was gay might not be the hardest thing in the world.

These thoughts, and thoughts about the assembly, had carried Ethan away in the wellness center for two days in a row, and then again on his walk with Jay. Suddenly, he felt exhausted, in a scary way. He spent the night battling an extreme case of nausea and a headache, desperately wanting to sleep, but not achieving it. He called Sophie in the morning to tell her that he wouldn't be able to come to the Y, and she came over right away, urging her friend to drink lots of fluids, bringing a container of soup for his lunch and, wanting to stay, but admitting that she was just too busy at work to do so.

When she left, she gave Ethan a pile of notes and pictures about the assembly, stuff she had brought from her office in case he wanted something to look at to take his mind off of his illness. It was an intriguing stack of images and words, and since the event was only a month away, it gave him an opportunity to curl up on the sofa with some tea so that he could read and rest at the same time.

The agenda mirrored some of the conference calls Ethan had heard Sophie on, with titles and themes that he recognized. Some of the names were also familiar because they had been frequent contributors on the phone. There was Pete from Dallas, Alison from Syracuse, Kate from Boise, Erica from Somerset Hills, and Dave from Tampa. These were the lead staff at the assembly, because they were also lead staff providing the foundations for the development of the LIVE**STRONG** at the YMCA initiative.

Sophie had many tales from the early days involving the growth and spread of the Y's cancer survivor work. Back then, the program's structure and communication systems had not been as polished—and so, as more and more Ys became involved, methods of sharing and helping were often rushed and stressful. She had some particular stories involving conference calls with fifty or sixty individuals on the line, often talking at once or being silent at once. On one occasion, a participant had put her phone on hold, and in Y's all around the country, elevator music had drifted out of speakerphones, drowning out efforts to hear or be heard.

Frustration had led to the development of regions, so that smaller groups of Ys could partner and share in a more manageable way key staff members—Kate, Alison, Erica, Dave, and Pete—had stepped forward to lead in each area of the country.

The paperwork Sophie had given Ethan was a mixture of informational and emotional data; facts and figures mixed in with photographs and stories. The focus on the first day of the conference was sustainability. The LIVE**STRONG** at the YMCA program was free to members, and so there was an economic burden immediately placed on the shoulders of a branch and its staff members when they took the program on. But the burden became light, easy to carry and worth carrying as tales and images of hope and laughter began to emerge from locker rooms and workout rooms, as yellow shirts and bandannas began appearing in the hallways of buildings old and new, putting a determined face on the healthy-living work that YMCAs were doing nationally.

The structure that Sophie had put in place for the conference reflected the two sides of LIVE**STRONG** at the YMCA. There were matters of importance to discuss: how members were retained, how funds were raised, what statistics could be gathered and how these statistics could be used.

Then there were equal matters of importance to listen to, look at, and revel in: emotional matters that could lead to a deeper understanding of, appreciation of, and connection to the personal nature of this work; essays written by survivors extolling the Y and its staff, describing in wondrous prose the physical and mental improvements that had been made in bodies and minds wracked by an awful disease; and photographs to match, depicting faces lined with character and uniqueness, united by optimism. These were words and images that hit home for Ethan, as he lay on the couch drained by his own bout of cancer, still hundreds of miles away from Austin.

In the middle of the pile, he found a folder with more still shots—so many pictures of smiling faces and laughter, of people displaying attitudes that seemed to strangle cancer through the power of will and the potency of friendship and hope. Individuals exercised but winked at the camera; groups met before class and linked arms, laughing harmoniously; more groups met outside the Y on field trips, lunch adventures, or hikes, waving banners and wearing shirts that said "unity is strength" or "attitude is everything."

In one snapshot, two older women in headscarves stood on either side of an embroidered flag on which someone, presumably one or both of the women, had painstakingly stitched the words of the LIVE**STRONG** Foundation manifesto. The picture had been enlarged, and the statement was easy to read:

> *We believe in life.*
> *Your life.*
> *We believe in living every minute of it with every ounce of your being.*
> *And that you must not let cancer take control of it.*
> *We believe in energy: channeled and fierce.*
> *We believe in focus: getting smart and living strong.*
> *Unity is strength. Knowledge is power. Attitude is everything.*
>
> *This is the LIVE**STRONG** Foundation.*
> *We kick in the moment you're diagnosed.*

We help you accept the tears. Acknowledge the rage.
We believe in your right to live without pain.
We believe in information. Not pity.
And in straight, open talk about cancer.
With husbands, wives, and partners. With kids, friends, and neighbors.
Your healthcare team. And the people you live with, work with, cry
and laugh with.
This is no time to pull punches.
You're in the fight of your life.

We're about the hard stuff.
Like finding the nerve to ask for a second opinion.
And a third, or a fourth, if that's what it takes.
We're about preventing cancer. Finding it early. Getting smart about
clinical trials.
And if it comes to it, being in control of how your life ends.
It's your life. You will have it your way.

We're about the practical stuff.
Planning for surviving. Banking your sperm. Preserving your fertility.
Organizing your finances. Dealing with hospitals, specialists, insurance
companies, and employers.
It's knowing your rights.
It's your life. Take no prisoners.

We're about the fight.
We're your advocate before policymakers. Your champion within the
healthcare system. Your sponsor in the research labs.
And we know the fight never ends.
Cancer may leave your body, but it never leaves your life.
*This is the LIVE**STRONG** Foundation.*
Founded and inspired by Lance Armstrong, one of the toughest cancer
survivors on the planet.

The words were designed to move and inspire, and Ethan had to read them again, and then had to pause to close his eyes. He was a writer and also a lover of art, and so had experienced the practical effects of poetry, prose, art, and music on the mind and soul. The manifesto was its own form of poetry, a speech and a song that obviously spoke to survivors and was speaking to him. The idea of the LIVE**STRONG** Foundation and its assembly, of a gathering of folks who could unify around the fight, really coalesced in his mind as he lay on the couch and recovered, reading more of Sophie's notes with interest.

Another topic on the second day caught his eye. It was a focus on cancer survivorship; exercise; and new initiatives, ideas, and research available in this field. Kate, a woman from Boise and one of Sophie's closest associates, was presenting the topic, together with a woman named Anna Schwartz. Ethan had heard she was a fascinating lady: Sophie had talked about her many times at regular intervals since becoming involved with LIVE**STRONG** at the YMCA. There was an old press clipping from *USA Today* in the bundle of assembly pages. It gave an overview of Anna and her work around cancer and exercise:

> When Anna Schwartz was having chemotherapy, there were days when she felt barely strong enough to climb out of bed. Still, she pushed herself to walk, jog, even play tennis while hooked up to a catheter.
>
> "I don't think exercise makes you think you are going to beat cancer, but it gives you the strength to push through it," says Schwartz, who survived several bouts with non-Hodgkin's lymphoma. "You think, 'If I go out and exercise today, I am going to feel better.'"
>
> Schwartz, author of *Cancer Fitness*, is one of a growing number of researchers who say exercise can provide a powerful healing tool for people going through cancer treatment and recovery.
>
> The National Cancer Institute has financed more than three dozen grants over the past three years to study physical

activity among cancer survivors, says Julia Rowland, director of the cancer survivorship office at NCI. "This is one of the hottest fields of research."

Exercise doesn't have to be organized or especially rigorous to do some good, research shows:

o A study in May in the *Journal of the American Medical Association* found that breast cancer survivors who walked three to five hours a week cut their risk of dying by half compared with sedentary women.

o Colon cancer patients who exercised regularly also were half as likely to die from the disease, according to research presented in May at the annual meeting of the American Society of Clinical Oncology.

o An analysis of 34 studies in the June 1 issue of the *Journal of Clinical Oncology* found that, on balance, cancer patients benefit from physical activity. Experts say that only large, carefully designed trials in which patients are randomly assigned to exercise can really prove that working out improves survival.

In her book, Schwartz says she hopes to puncture the "myth of rest." Too often, cancer patients are told to "take it easy," she says.

Patients end up spending their days on the couch. Their bones weaken, their muscles atrophy, and their stamina disappears, leaving them too weak to carry out daily chores. Many become depressed.

Exercise, on the other hand, combats fatigue by helping patients keep up their strength, Schwartz says. Exercise can lift patients' moods and help them feel better about their bodies, which can be especially important for people who are disfigured by their illness or treatment.

"People may think, 'I have cancer, but I'm walking farther than I've ever done, I'm running, I'm swimming,' and they're delighted with themselves," Schwartz says. "They never imagined they could be doing what they are doing." Working out with other cancer survivors can be especially powerful, "like a support group that moves."

It was an interesting article that added a level of professional and personal knowledge to Sophie's descriptions about Anna. Ethan's friend had talked about Dr. Schwartz as a world-class cyclist and an expert in the area of exercise and cancer survivorship, but had really focused on the woman's humor and levels of empathy and sympathy—especially the humor.

Sophie often told the story of one of Anna's first-ever PowerPoint presentations to their group, in the early days of the development of the LIVE**STRONG** at the YMCA effort, when Y staff members had been new to cancer survivorship. She had been giving a very serious talk on the science of exercise and cancer when suddenly, up popped a picture of a horse doing what looked like a choreographed dance move. More science, and then, another picture of a horse. Each time the horse appeared, Dr. Schwartz would pause and, with amazing dryness, describe the particular move the animal was performing, as though it was the most natural thing in the world to mix horse artistry in with cancer.

The discipline apparently was called "reining," a sport that involved the rider taking his or her mount through an intricate series of circles, spins, and stops. Anna excelled in reining and perhaps loved it more than cycling, which was as good a reason as any to sneak slides into a presentation. When Sophie told the story, she marveled at the way Anna was able to pass on an enormous amount of knowledge in a short amount of time using a very special brand of insight, expertise, and a relaxed teaching style. Stirring in pictures of reining was just her sense of humor. Ethan was looking forward to meeting her.

The assembly agenda was punctuated with a LIVE**STRONG** Foundation "State of the Foundation" luncheon on Thursday and a Mission Collaborative meeting on Friday morning, the latter of which would involve all of the agencies present, not just the Y. Sophie had praised the level of organization at the 2011 event, and also complimented the way the foundation presented itself. She said the focus lay on the frontline organizations, those that had been funded and were doing the work in the communities, and not on the LIVE**STRONG** Foundation itself. She said that last year Doug Ulman, the president and chief executive officer, had made a point of saying that the foundation did not want to expand, did not want to be the biggest or the most widespread cancer survivor serving agency. Instead, the LIVE**STRONG** Foundation wanted to stay in Austin to raise funds, so that it could help grassroots volunteers help survivors around the country and around the world.

There was a lot of information to digest, and while Ethan was feeling better after his exertions of the previous two days, he was still tired. He decided to lie on his bed with the stack of photographs to flick through and admire, so that he could fall asleep with practical examples of hope lying on his chest.

22

There were days when it felt like Ethan's cancer journey was about taking one step forward and one step back. Both, it seemed, were a necessary part of the voyage, ingrained in the DNA of recovery.

The extra state of exhaustion he had experienced, thankfully, seemed to be just that—an extraordinary state brought about by his overreaching. After a few days of rest and a diet of fresh fruit, veggies, and soup delivered by his friend, he felt okay, and was back to exercising. In fact, after a few sessions of exercise were behind him, he felt good overall.

Ethan's strength definitely seemed to be improving gradually, as was his endurance, and the general attitude and condition of his group was upbeat. Sophie had a mantra that had been reflected in the article about Anna Schwartz: that exercising was part physical and part mental, and the ratio of the parts differed from person to person. Individuals could definitely increase their levels of strength, endurance, and flexibility using exercise while going through cancer treatments or recovering from cancer, and that was a good thing, something that helped the body withstand the strains of the disease and the treatments. But there was also something empowering about just *doing* something while fighting cancer, about a survivor being encouraged to exercise or encouraging him or herself to take charge in some way. It felt good to try. Then add the fact that the trying involved other people in a fun, friendly, public place, out of the house, out of the hospital—and many of the ingredients needed for recovery were there.

Ethan could see these effects in his LIVE**STRONG** at the YMCA group. As the weather gradually changed outside, so this collection of cancer survivors seemed to change inside. On one particular day, he saw transformation all around. Suzie had taken her wig off to avoid sweating and had a yellow bandanna wrapped around her head. She was matched with Anne, and both women were working on their legs—focused and pushing themselves one minute, and then laughing out loud at some joke or observation the next. Brenda and Norma were together doing their arms, and the level of confidence on display in both women was impressive— especially since Brenda had been advised to be extra careful with exercising her upper body, since her breast cancer had required surgery and the removal of some lymph nodes.

Lymphedema was one of the buzzwords and one of the scariest aspects of working with cancer survivors for the Y staff. It was a condition most frequently seen after lymph node dissection, surgery, and/or radiation therapy, in which damage to the lymphatic system was caused during the treatment of cancer, most often breast cancer. Pictures Sophie had shown her friend highlighted parts of the body—mainly the arms, legs, or feet— swollen because the lymphatic system was not working correctly and the lymph fluid had collected in one area of the body, causing it to swell. Brenda knew of the concern, but also knew that she wanted to get stronger—and so she continued to work out, being careful to follow modified exercises that Jenny had given her for the right side of her body.

So there was success, fulfillment, and happiness among the LIVE**STRONG** at the YMCA group in the wellness center, except for the fact that Dave was missing. It was not unusual for one of the group to be absent at any time because of the nature of their conditions, but also because many of them had family lives or jobs that needed their attention.

Ethan had been thinking about going to the membership desk to call Dave to see if everything was okay when Sophie came in, crying, headed straight for him, and just leaned against his shoulder, sobbing.

The rest of the people in the group saw her and came over, concerned, as did some of the regular YMCA members that knew Sophie. Eventually, she slowed down enough to tell everyone that Dave's son had died earlier that morning, finally succumbing to a terrible bout of cancer. Mary had just called to let the Y staff know.

The news was heartbreaking because it was Dave and Mary, because it was somebody's son, and because they had all met Josh. There were shocked faces and tears all around, until Jenny led her group out and into a small conference room where they could have some privacy. She looked distraught herself, but was composed enough to tell everyone to sit and take deep breaths and that when someone was ready, that person could talk and express what they were feeling. There was relative silence for a few minutes, with just the sound of Brenda gently crying in a corner. So Ethan decided he would try to start, since he had been Dave's training buddy and felt like he had begun to get to know him.

He talked about how Dave had often said that seeing his son go through cancer was so much harder than going through it himself. As Ethan and Dave had gotten to know each other and exercised together, he had gradually told stories of Josh growing up; and as was the case with every growing boy and teenager, some tales were good, others not so good. The love he had for his only child was evident, as was the pain he felt when he described living through Josh's diagnosis, and also seeing the ravaging toll that liver cancer, which seemed to be one of the worst strains of the disease, had on a member of his own family. Seeing someone so young physically and emotionally decimated and having that young person be one's own son was too much.

But Dave's discovery of the LIVE**STRONG** at the YMCA program had been a powerful spirit-lifter, providing him with a means to recover physically while seeing and helping others recover physically. Dave was a very social man when sadness was not consuming him, and his time at the Y with friends kept the depression at bay.

Mary, Dave's wife and Josh's mother, had said on a number of occasions that the Y had given her back her own life as well. She had continuously marveled at how energetic and happy her husband was, and that, in turn, had caused a burden to fall from her heart. She told Ethan that Dave's depression was mostly due to his son's condition, more than his own health issues. Mary had talked about the things they had once done together, the activities and trips, how close they had been, but that Dave's illness and then their son's cancer had taken away his personality and zest for life. He would just sit in the house and watch TV all day, and then sleep—until they found the LIVE**STRONG** at the YMCA program. It was only then that he had begun to come alive again, even though his son's condition had continued to be critical. That had been the true miracle.

There was a fresh round of tears as Ethan spoke, and then emotion brought him to a sudden halt. Suzie began talking quickly to keep the sharing going. She admitted she had not known all of Dave's background, but was surprised to hear that he had ever been depressed. She said that when she closed her eyes, the picture she imagined was Dave's smile, and in particular, his smile when he was around his wife. His whole face lit up in Mary's presence, and Suzie couldn't imagine how devastating this was for both of them.

In the end, most of those present shared a thought or memory, and even though the closed-door session was brief, when it ended everyone seemed to have a vision of how they could move forward, how they could help. There was still sadness, but the common theme that had come out of the sharing was that Dave and Mary's experiences with their fellow survivors and with the Y over the last few months had been happy and helpful, and the group, as a team, needed to find out how they could support them—and, if possible, bring them back into the fold soon.

23

Many stories Ethan had heard and read described the cancer survivor's journey as a roller coaster ride. Even though he now felt he was plummeting downward, he tried to think good thoughts, and good thoughts came to him when he was outside and with his dog.

One of the reasons Ethan went to Honeymoon Island so often was because it made him relax to see his dog happy, free, running around, sniffing, and exercising. People were not supposed to let their dogs off the leash anywhere on the island, but many people did, then just shrugged and said sorry when a park ranger appeared. Jay was pretty smart and obedient, too. He responded well to his master whistling. Ethan had a special, sharp note he let out if a ranger was around. That was Jay's cue to race back to be put on the leash. Usually, this worked—but even when it didn't, and the park staff spotted his dog, they were so impressed with his obedience and friendliness that they were never harsh with their rebukes.

Even though he was relaxed and enjoying the fresh air and his dog was at play, Ethan was still in shock, still sad to think that Dave's son was gone. If he was honest, the sadness came in different shades: dark because Dave was a friend and such a nice man; and darker still because Josh had been a cancer survivor, and a selfish side of Ethan was discouraged by the fact that a man he knew, who lived nearby, could die of cancer. If it could happen to Josh, it could happen to him. In fact, death was as likely to happen to him as it was to Josh: the type of cancer Ethan had was potent, and statistically, he had a fifty percent chance of pulling through.

A new movie called *50-50* had been made about a young man finding out that he had cancer and then going through the stages of recovery. Sophie and Ethan had gone to see it because it had been well reviewed and because it had a happy ending. It had been good, very good—well acted, funny, touching, and well written. It had been created by a producer who had just been through cancer himself, which was why the story had felt so real.

What was interesting was that the main effect the film had on Ethan was not related to cancer. The protagonist's efforts to cope with the disease had been the crux of the movie, and that definitely made him think, because he was still going through treatment and was not sure if he would recover. But the main hook for Ethan revolved around the love interest, and the fact that the film ended with the main character beginning a relationship with a young woman he had met and befriended during treatment.

The woman had been his counselor, helping him through some of the psychological aspects of cancer recovery, and the interactions they had as he struggled with his disease and the personal revelations he had made as he looked for help had drawn them closer together as the plot moved on. It was pretty clear, as the credits rolled, that this man had met his future wife, his soul mate.

One of the brightest aspects of Dave's fight with cancer involved his wife Mary, a woman who so adored him and whom Dave adored in return. It was easy for Ethan to close his eyes and picture her looking through the wellness center window as Dave exercised, so much love in her smile—and Ethan could see Dave's face when he noticed her looking, the big grin and the unashamedly blown kiss. They were so made for each other.

Part of him wondered at the wisdom of admitting to anyone else that he was gay, or of completely accepting the fact himself. Not, of course, that he had a choice in the matter, but not only did he not have any positive experiences in any kind of relationship at all, he really had no experience finding and forming the kind of relationship that was still frowned upon by many. The two relationships he'd been in had both come when he was in college, that mosh pit of emotions, hormones, and experimental hook-ups, and both times, the guys involved had been the ones to initiate things.

How could he meet people now, when he was not cocooned in an educational establishment with thousands of other individuals? How would he even get to talk to someone who might have an interest in forming a relationship? Should he put an ad in a local single's paper? Should he go on Match.com? Was he just supposed to hope whenever he went out the door that he would meet his soul mate? It all seemed so hard. He wondered why he had never asked Dave how he and his wife had met, and vowed to do that next time they were together. He imagined that the story behind their relationship would be full of romance, full of chance and luck. Ethan wondered if he could possibly have so much luck, enough to pull him through his illness and then on to a disease-free other side, and enough to find a partner for life. That seemed like an awful lot of luck.

He now purposefully carried around the book that his former-editor friend Tony had recommended so that, whenever he thought he was going through a tough time, he could read about Marc. Ethan could not imagine being so young and getting diagnosed with cancer. Sitting on Honeymoon Island and contemplating life and love, he pulled out the paperback and read the introduction again, the young man's cancer timeline.

My life in brief

SUMMER 1985
One Saturday, at the start of my summer holidays, my ankle becomes swollen and is painful to walk on. The most energetic things I had done were to drink a cup of tea and watch television. Over the following months I go through numerous diagnostic processes and am eventually told that, aged sixteen, I have a type of arthritis.

CHRISTMAS 1986
For over a year I hobble around, my left ankle gradually getting worse and starting to collapse. A new round of appointments with specialists and doctors begins. When I'm

sent for a bone biopsy, I realize that whatever is happening must be pretty serious. By this time, I just want to find out what is wrong. Two weeks before Christmas, I find out. I have cancer.

I have to have my leg amputated. Christmas flies by, punctuated by gatherings of concerned-looking family members and more tests, this time at an oncology centre. I spend a lot of time thinking about what I will and won't be able to do in the future as an amputee.

NEW YEAR 1987
My first five-day-long chemotherapy session straddles the New Year celebrations. On the afternoon that I enter the hospital, I still have very little idea of what chemotherapy might feel like, or what it will mean to me.

Within six hours of starting the treatment, I understand the language of chemotherapy. The cancer might kill me in the long run, but the chemotherapy feels like it is trying to kill me right now.

JANUARY 1987
Amputation day approaches: 20 January 1987.

Talking to my father before the operation, I want to find something I am able to do with one leg. Swimming seems to be the answer. I was a county swimmer before and I should be able to swim with one leg. Perhaps there are competitions especially for amputees. Before I even have my operation, my father enters me for the National Swimming Championships for the Disabled the following June!

The amputation happens and I deal with it in my own way. The pain is not as all-consuming as I feared, but the phantom pains are both alarming and unpleasant. I celebrate my 18th birthday on 1 February, at the mercy of my phantom pains.

JANUARY–JUNE 1987
The chemotherapy continues to grind away at me, sapping

my strength, testing my resolve.

Meanwhile, I have my artificial limb fitted.

MAY 1987

Outside the cancer ward, I'm desperate to keep hold of some level of normality. I go to see the school compete at a swimming gala.

JUNE 1987

By the time I finish my treatment, I am literally half the man I used to be. I have lost both weight and a limb.

I compete at the National Disabled Swimming Championships, which my father had entered me for six months previously. Surprisingly, I win three medals. I've come out the other end of the tunnel fighting. It's a fight I vow to carry on.

JUNE 1987 ONWARDS

Swimming becomes an even bigger focus for me once I finish my treatment. Soon I am swimming faster with one leg than I once did with two.

OCTOBER 1988

Eighteen months after finishing my chemotherapy, I'm good enough and lucky enough to represent Great Britain at the Seoul Paralympics. I win two gold medals, one silver medal, and two bronze medals, a feat I consider to be pretty respectable. I have turned my life around—from the "deathbed" to the podium—in a relatively short time and both my family and I are thrilled.

1988–2000

For the next twelve years, swimming is my priority. My father, who had taught me to swim when I was four, coached me when I went to Seoul. Now, when I go to university, I take on a new coach. I finish my degree, but it is the swimming that drives me on, and with my parents there as my number one fans, I win medals at both Barcelona and Atlanta.

OCTOBER 2000

I set my sights on competing in my fourth Games in Sydney and adding to my gold medal collection. All preparations are going well and the 4x100m freestyle relay team, which I'm part of, looks on track to win the gold at Sydney. Then, just two days before I am due to fly out, my father unexpectedly dies of a massive stroke, aged just fifty-seven. I cancel my flight and, along with my brother, help my Mum to organize the funeral and deal with all the awful paperwork.

The family is shattered. I want to be with my Mum and help her. But after discussing it, we decide that I really should go to Sydney. My father would have been furious with himself if he knew he was the reason why I didn't go.

And so, the day after his funeral, I take the long, lonely flight to Sydney—one of the hardest things I have ever done. My teammates are there for me and help me through an awful situation. The race is a memorable one. The BBC's Stuart Storey ranks it as his highlight of the games. We win the gold. It is both the best and the worst week of my life.

2004 ATHENS

The relay team is victorious once again, which brings my Paralympic medal tally up to twelve. As I climb out of the pool, I take some time to look back across the water and over to the spectators. I quietly say goodbye to that part of my life, then collect my things and walk away under the grandstand.

2008 BEIJING

By now we know that London will host the London 2012 Olympic and Paralympic Games. I take on a new challenge: commentating for the BBC. It feels strange not to be competing, I make plenty of mistakes, but enjoy the whole experience as Great Britain has a very successful Games.

TODAY

I am no longer a competitive swimmer, but I have taken on new challenges. I have my own motivational speaking business, and a business consultancy. I also work with the Teenage Cancer Trust and the Youth Sport Trust, both of which do fantastic work to enhance the lives of young people. The biggest change for me, though, has been that I am now a husband and a father, which, as for everyone, brings its own challenges. So now, as I attempt to spin many plates, I often find myself thinking about my father, and that if I can even get close to being half the man he was, I will be doing well.

Tony Cannavaro had met this young man, had interviewed Marc Woods for a magazine story he had written. He had said Marc was inspirational in person, and his story was certainly moving. If a boy could go through the trials that he had experienced and come out the other side determined and successful, then there was certainly hope—especially considering Ethan didn't want to be an Olympic athlete, didn't want to be an inspirational speaker and didn't want to be on television. Like Marc, he wanted to be cancer-free, wanted to survive, but unlike Marc, he would be happy to settle for everyday success, not world-class success. Also, more and more, he wanted to share that success with someone he loved.

He had spoken to Tony, calling to let him know how he was and thanking him for the book recommendation. Yet again, he was impressed that this big man with a big, Italian persona, who had made his name writing about vicious Mafia dons and thugs, was so thoughtful and caring. Tony asked a lot of questions about Ethan's cancer, his treatment, his mental state, and how he was coping. Then he talked about Ethan's writing and whether he would be interested in pursuing it again. He said that the journalism business was not in a great place at the moment, but there was still room for good writers with good ideas, and his company was beginning to come to terms with the online world and the business model for being involved in it. He was interested in the writing Ethan had been doing during his cancer journey, thought it might make a good blog piece, and asked him to e-mail a sample. He wasn't offering money yet—just his interest.

So that gave Ethan hope beyond cancer. The thought of focusing on writing was exciting. To have a career in writing—that was a long-term road he could see himself walking down. Being a writer was part of his inner self, one of his many "selves" that had been hidden for so long but might yet be revealed. Perhaps this literary revelation might follow closely on the tail of a more personal revelation in Austin, Texas.

Ethan had decided not to discuss his sexuality with the **LIVESTRONG** at the YMCA group yet. Sophie had asked him about that, wondering if part of the process of coming to terms with who he really was would be helped by talking openly in an environment that he trusted, in a group where he felt safe. Ethan had thought about it, but decided not to. His thinking was that cancer was enough; they all had overflowing plates already without him throwing out another issue to consider. It felt selfish. The time didn't feel right.

One night, weeks earlier, Ethan had pulled out an old documentary he had on DVD that covered Lance's triumphs in the Tour de France. As he watched it, he remembered watching it as a younger man and being impressed and excited, willing this freakish athlete, this American, to do the unthinkable and become the best in the world in the world's own backyard. And as he watched the reruns, he also remembered that as he had admired Lance all those years ago, he had also been attracted to him, with the repressed attraction of a man in his mid-thirties who was by then used to repression. Then, Ethan had been a screwed-up, introverted accountant; and now he was a screwed-up, introverted accountant, wannabe writer, and cancer survivor. He couldn't wait for the **LIVESTRONG** Assembly. More and more, his expectation was that the experience was going to heal him—at least psychologically.

24

~

Sophie was so impressed with Ethan's efforts in so many areas of his life that one day, she bought him a bike—and presented it in a very unique way. One of the more meaningful aspects of LIVE**STRONG** at the YMCA was that, while it was focused on exercise and helping cancer survivors regain their strength, endurance, and flexibility, the program was also focused on overall wellness. Of course, wellness might mean different things to different people, but from a YMCA perspective, an important aspect of wellness involved making personal connections and developing relationships.

So Sophie and Jenny made a point of organizing social gatherings based upon the likes and interests of their group or of individuals in their group, in addition to the twice-a-week exercise program. Over the years, they had made visits to a local pottery studio to make vases, gone on picnics to local parks, visited a local aquarium, and even gone to the circus. All of these activities had involved the children and spouses of participants to make sure family members were not left out of the cancer recovery process.

One sunny Thursday, at noon, Ethan had gone to the Y, ready to ride his reliable upright bike and lift some weights. Just inside the automatic doors, in the lobby of the Y, all of his friends and several staff members were standing, waiting. They applauded as they saw him. Sophie was in the middle of the crowd and she was holding up a piece of carbon fiber that rivaled her own beauty: a Pinarello racing bike. It was white with red writing on the frame, shiny, polished, sleek, fast, and worth much too much—certainly more than Sophie should have been spending on a gift.

Ethan was speechless, but he had no time to begin to look for words because his classmates led him outside, around a corner, and to the back of the Y, where family members waited, holding an array of bikes: some racing, some mountain, some utility, and some small bikes for kids. The social that day was going to mix exercise with Florida climate appreciation and a large helping of social time; they were going on a group ride.

Sophie had set up Ethan's bike based on guesswork, and he adjusted the seat and handlebars a little before they left. It was to be a short ride: down 16th Street to Pennsylvania, a right on Pennsylvania to Omaha, right on Omaha to Alderman, a right to Westlake, and then gently through the subdivision to that housing community's clubhouse, where they were going to have a picnic. Even though it was an easy distance, the group still stopped a couple of times to make sure each individual was comfortable, not adversely affected by a different form of exercise in the Florida heat.

Ethan felt like the years had fallen away, like he was healthy and young, ready to race his father down Woodward Avenue. He put on a little speed going down Omaha past the high school, and it felt like someone else was doing the work, like he was gliding. When he thought about riding a bike, dreamed about riding a bike, this was what it felt like.

They got to the Westlake Village clubhouse all too quickly, and Ethan had to swallow a growing bundle of energy and desire, forcing himself off of the Pinarello so that they could all sit and eat on a set of picnic tables in the sun. His friends had been in high spirits, as they always were when they did something different, something to change up the routine. The bike ride was special because it really felt like recovery, due to the exercise, the energy they expended, the muscles they used—but in particular, because they had done it in the fresh air and surrounded by family, laughing and joking as a team. Each of the survivors had had moments when they were alone in a bed, in pain, thinking about death, so to be eating good food with good friends out in the sunshine felt special.

Ethan had not had enough of his new bike, though. When they rode back to the Y, his friends left to do different things, and Sophie had to go back to work. After he gave her a huge thank-you hug, they loaded the bike into his car, a fairly roomy hatchback, and he told her he was going home to rest.

Ethan did go home to put his car in the garage—but then he headed back out on the bike down to the Pinellas Trail.

The trail was designed for walkers, runners, and bikers, and stretched from St. Petersburg in the south all the way up north to Tarpon Springs. It was a great resource, because while the roads in the area were pretty bike friendly, they were also full of snowbirds, senior citizens who traveled down to soak up some Florida sunshine in the winter, when it was cold and bleak up North.

It was a joke in the area that, from around November to March, driving on US 19, a major north-to-south road through Pinellas County, was like buying a lottery ticket. Driving at a steady fifty miles an hour, one could encounter a car in the fast lane going twenty that would suddenly spot a restaurant of interest and swerve across four other lanes to get to the parking lot, sending cars weaving and braking, with drivers cursing and laying on their horns in its wake.

Of course, there were also excellent older drivers, but it only took one or two to cause an accident. These seniors often made the wise decision to stay off the major roads, but that meant that biking on a minor road on a hard-to-see vehicle, even in a bike lane, could be dangerous, too.

The Pinellas Trail was an exercising paradise, and while walkers and runners used it, the trail was well marked and rules were respected, so bikers could get up some speed safely. That had been Ethan's intention. He was on an Italian-made piece of precision machinery, and to inch along keeping pace with recreational riders, even though those riders were his friends, seemed like a crime. He wanted to open this baby up—and did so as soon as he saw some free pathway ahead of him.

The objective was to head up toward Tarpon Springs, away from the busiest areas in Dunedin and Clearwater, to maybe hit Tarpon Avenue, and then turn around. It was a quiet part of the day, warm but with some clouds in the sky, so there were a few walkers, the odd jogger, and a couple of cyclists that Ethan cruised by with ease. The bike was such a smooth ride, gears changing quietly, wheels turning effortlessly. He looked ahead, focusing on the path, but in his ears he had "Paradise" by Coldplay thumping loudly, and in his mind he was in a pack of riders on the Champs-Élysées, with crowds roaring his name. After nearly an hour, he didn't even notice the sweat soaking his shirt.

Apparently, he also didn't notice the dark ledge of consciousness over which he quietly rode.

Ethan woke up in a hospital bed, with Sophie sitting next to him reading a book. When he groaned, she looked over, smiled, and slowly shook her head. She asked how he was feeling, told him he was stupid, and then asked him to guesstimate how much trouble she was in. He was still groggy and not sure where he was and how he had made it there, but Sophie had an ax to grind, and grind it she did.

Apparently, a walker had found Ethan lying unconscious on the trail next to his bike and had quickly called 911. Then she'd tried the "in case of emergency" number Ethan had in his phone. Sophie had made it to the scene just as the paramedics were hooking her friend up to an IV and loading him into an ambulance to take him to the emergency room. She, of course, was concerned on a personal level, but also had to call the incident in to her boss, the chief operating officer of the YMCA of the Suncoast, who had been astounded when Sophie told her Ethan had been riding a bike that she had given to him as a present. Apparently, her boss had asked her at least three times, "Why did you give a cancer survivor in treatment a bike? Tell me one more time, why did you give a cancer survivor in treatment a brand new racing bike?"

Groggy or not, Ethan did feel incredibly selfish, and apologized with such obvious sincerity that Sophie told him to be quiet and rest. She actually let him rest for about two minutes before railing again, asking whether he had drunk any liquids before getting on his bike, how far he'd thought he was going to go on his bike, whether he actually understood the difference between riding in an air-conditioned YMCA and riding outside in the mid-afternoon Florida heat, and if he remembered how he had oh-so-recently suffered exhaustion from overdoing it. She was brutal, mopped her friend's brow with a damp cloth, was brutal again, and then gave him a sip of cold water.

Ethan spent the next hour dozing in and out. At some point he noticed that Sophie got up from the bed to answer a phone call. When she came back, her face looked white and shocked.

She sat quickly on the bed and took his hand. "Ethan, that was my boss again. She found out you're going to the assembly as our guest, and she says she won't allow it. She says she feels bad, and knows how important the assembly is to you, but she's concerned about liability, considering your condition. I'll call the foundation, but I'm not optimistic. Invitees only come as part of funded organizations, so I don't think you could go on your own."

Ethan didn't know how to react, could say nothing. He just looked up at Sophie as she apologized again and again.

25

He had to stay in the hospital overnight while he was rehydrated, but eventually Ethan was released to go back home, with strict instructions from the doctor on duty, and from Sophie, to rest. He didn't need much persuasion—he felt like he'd been hit in the back of his head with a brick. He had a pounding headache and just felt weak. He did wonder what he had been thinking, understood that he had been excited by the look and feel of a new bike—but acknowledged to himself again that he had been stupid. Really stupid, in fact, because now his dream, his motivation, was over.

Fate was, it seemed, inexorable: while Ethan was resting he had a call from his oncologist, admonishing him for his decision to ride a bike in the Florida humidity. The oncologist also said it was time to come in for follow-up tests, to see how Ethan's body was reacting to chemotherapy, and in particular, to see how chemotherapy was dealing with the cancer. His appointment was set for Wednesday, April 4, four days after the assembly—the assembly that he was not attending anymore.

He had thought about asking if he could get the scan earlier, to ease his mind and release the building tension, but decided against it for two reasons. Number one: what if the test results were bad? No way would the Y let him go then. The second reason was less rational, perverse even, but Ethan felt that he actually needed the threat of cancer hovering over him to help him focus, to give him urgency. He realized too late that the prospect of immersing himself in the mission and hope of the foundation had been keeping him afloat, buoying him up and allowing him to move forward, change, and improve, even as a disease gnawed away at his body and mind.

Having a test date meant a clock had started ticking in Ethan's mind, ticking louder and louder, a repetitive reminder that he would soon find out if he still had cancer or not. Had remnants of the disease really been left behind when the tumor was removed? Had it spread before the operation? Had the chemotherapy wiped the disease out while it was wiping Ethan out?

And to compound his worries, had fate changed? Had his foolish decision to ride a bike alone in the heat taken him off onto a different path, off the path from Detroit to Clearwater to Austin, and onto one that led to more sickness, more loneliness, more sadness? Ethan needed to find a way to Texas before he got the results of his tests—because success bred success, didn't it? Fate had led him to Sophie, to cancer, to the YMCA, to the LIVE**STRONG** Foundation, and the rest of the story was Austin, health, and happiness. Wasn't it?

Turmoil raged in his mind for what seemed like hours, until Ethan sought the only refuge available to a bedridden, sick man—he turned on the TV. He flipped the channels through mindless images until he eventually found something to focus on.

Satellite television had turned him into a soccer fan. Ethan had never played the game, and it had never interested him until he saw his first English Premier League game on the Fox Soccer channel. It was the crowd noise that drew him in initially, rather than the game itself: the constant hum of oohs and aahs, and the singing, along with the intricacy and musicality of the songs. They were not just everyday chants—a "let's go" here or a rip-off of a '70s rock anthem there—but were original lyrical verses sung by thousands of raucous, enraptured fans.

The game Ethan found to drown out his anxiety was again on the Fox Soccer channel. It involved the prestigious Champions League, a competition that pitted the best teams in Europe against each other. Games were decided by an aggregate score from two matches, home and away, and the English team on display, Arsenal, had been thrashed four to nothing in Italy against the equally renowned AC Milan. But now, in the second leg, as he watched, Arsenal scored three goals in the first half alone.

The English had a Dutchman playing for them, Robin van Persie, who was just in a different class as a striker, and he scored one goal and set another up. But in the second half, the tension in the stadium matched the tension in Ethan's own house, as chance after chance was missed. Arsenal needed one more score to make it four to four and take the game into overtime, but it would not come—and then, there was the final whistle.

The game had calmed Ethan. Maybe watching a team that was down four to nothing battle back to be only one behind had soothed his fears a little. Maybe listening to a passionate crowd sing songs and roar encouragement to its team even though that team faced an uphill battle, a deficit that had never been overcome once in history—maybe that had helped him settle. But what made him smile and sigh and wonder was the final act in the game, an act that had come down from the terraces.

There was a great sports saying with an origin attributed to many commentators, but with a history firmly in Italian opera: "It ain't over till the fat lady sings"—meaning, keep trying because you never know what might happen until the final whistle blows. Over the years, Ethan had developed a love of opera, a love that had grown in direct correlation to his loneliness. Sophie was a great friend, but she had her own life, and often he needed to find things to do by himself. One day, his company had received free tickets to the Florida Orchestra, based in St. Petersburg, and since nobody had wanted them, he had gone and fallen in love with Mozart's *The Marriage of Figaro*.

After that, Ethan had bought season tickets and gone to many musical productions, one of which was Richard Wagner's opera suite *Der Ring des Nibelungen*. The last part of this production, "Götterdämmerung," was the section typically thought to have inspired the meaning of the saying "It ain't over till the fat lady sings." The "fat lady" is the Valkyrie Brünnhilde, traditionally presented as a very buxom lady with a horned helmet, spear, and round shield. Her singing piece lasts almost twenty minutes and leads directly to the end of the opera. As "Götterdämmerung" portrayed the end of the world—or at least the world of the Norse gods—"It ain't over 'til the fat lady sings" was apt in more ways than one.

As Ethan had watched the conclusion of the game, with three minutes to go and Arsenal still down by one and trying desperately to score, the traveling AC Milan fans, probably 2,000 of them, had started singing the most famous chorus from "Götterdämmerung"—opera on the terraces. The fat lady was singing, and it was all over for Arsenal.

But not for Ethan, perhaps. As the final notes of "Götterdämmerung" were fading away, his doorbell rang. Ethan staggered up, still sore and stiff, to answer it—and found Brenda, Steve, and Suzanne standing in the doorway, smiling.

He was surprised, not even sure how they knew where he lived, but very moved and happy at the same time. His three fellow survivors made their way through the door, passed the licks and wags of Jay, and settled themselves in the living room to talk.

Initially, of course, they wanted to know how Ethan was, what doctors and nurses had said, how the bike ride had gone, what had happened, and how he was feeling—mentally, more than physically. The underlying implication was that they knew about the assembly and knew he wasn't going.

"Sophie talked to us, told us what was going on." Steve was grinning as he spoke, and Ethan noticed that the man really did have a nice smile, all teeth and meaning, the latter of which shone from his eyes as well. "She wanted us to see you, to make sure you were okay. But she also thought we might be able to help with the situation. By the way, man, nice decision to ride off into the sunset on that cool bike."

Brenda started laughing so hard that she seemed to have difficulty stopping.

Their presence gave Ethan perspective again and made him smile. Here were three cancer survivors with their own fears and doubts, but they had pushed them aside for a friend and for a dream. Sophie was right: friendships, relationships, connections really were the foundation stones on which to build a happy life. Ethan was happy as Brenda laughed and Suzanne smiled and Steve shook his head, bemused. None of his problems had been solved, but many seemed as though they had—because he was not alone.

"Seriously, Ethan, we've called our people and our people have called their people, and we think it's going to be alright." Steve was now laughing, too.

"What do you mean you've called your people? Who do you know that can fix this?"

Suzie stood, came over, and gave him a big kiss on the lips. "Ethan, you've heard this a few times, I know. Seriously, the LIVE**STRONG** Foundation serves cancer survivors and no one but cancer survivors. With all due respect to Sophie's boss, who I know was trying to do the right thing for the Y, she can't stop you coming to the assembly. She isn't a cancer survivor; you are."

"Dude, we called our people." Brenda clearly became hyper-excited when she was making things happen—Ethan had never heard her use the term "dude" before. "I called some friends at the American Cancer Society, and they called the LIVE**STRONG** Foundation. Steve called his buddies who are LIVE**STRONG** leaders; did he tell you he was a LIVE**STRONG** leader? Anyway, they called the LIVE**STRONG** Foundation.

"And Suzie, well Suzie's the bad-ass here, because she called her congresswoman, who happens to be a multiple myeloma survivor, and *she* called the LIVE**STRONG** Foundation. Apparently she got through to the CEO himself.

"Bottom line: you're going to the assembly as a guest of the foundation, so the Y doesn't have to worry if you do something stupid down there and end up in hospital, like you did something stupid up here to end up in hospital. It's all on the foundation!"

Steve gave Brenda a big hug next to him on the couch and all three of Ethan's friends whooped with excitement. He had no idea if they understood why he wanted to go to the assembly, the meaning it had. Whether they did or didn't, they were happy, and they had helped him, and that meant more than anything.

26

E than was in a surrealistic place, a focused yet hazy dimension that he had never visited before—that few had visited before. It was a reality inhabited only by the drug-affected, the death-affected, fantasists, realists, and those tortured by doubt or hope. He was dying and he was living, dreaming, yet more lucid than he had ever been. Perhaps there were hundreds of individuals in his position, flying into Austin with the same sense of confusion and giddiness that he had.

The assembly had arrived. Ethan was flying alone because Sophie had left the day before. She was going to meet the leaders of a new group of associations involved in LIVE**STRONG** at the YMCA: Ys that had just finished the six-month learning process that prepared them to begin the program. Some of their final work had been timed to happen in Texas and to finish as the assembly started, so she was there and Ethan was flying solo.

Sophie had been so excited when she got the phone call confirming that he was officially registered—or rather, officially registered again. She said her boss was excited, too, and Ethan believed that. He had no problem with leaders being careful, especially leaders who were being careful with the YMCA when the Y had given so much to him.

His friend had also been excited to hear about the visit from Brenda, Suzie, and Steve. "Ethan, you know I didn't ask them to do all of that. I wanted to tell them what was going on, your condition and then your mental condition, because you were no longer going to the assembly. They did everything from there with no suggestion from me."

About halfway to Austin, though, Ethan began to get nervous. He had leaned his seat back to try to relax and understand exactly why he was nervous. It seemed to have arisen from a combination of factors—not least of which was the fact that this trip represented the culmination of a dream, a hope that an occasion might be powerful enough, spiritually and mentally meaningful enough, to make him well in many ways.

Of course, the assembly was meant to give Ethan the strength to face his upcoming scans, which would tell him whether his cancer had indeed spread and was still spreading, or whether the treatment he was receiving had been effective in combating the disease. But it was also supposed to give him the strength to be a more secure cancer survivor and a more secure person, to be honest with himself and others. It was meant to give him the self-assurance to move on as an openly gay man, to find the soul mate he was looking for and felt he needed so that he could be the person he wanted to be and make the difference he desired to make in the world. Ethan, too, wanted to feel the obligation of the cured and he wanted to take that obligation with him to New York, to Fat-Fingered Tony, who would help him write both for himself and others.

But he had done a remarkably stupid thing a few days after his trip to the assembly was secured—and it was that stupid thing that was making him nervous.

Ethan had been suckered into a drinking session with Sophie, even though she could handle her drink and he couldn't. He didn't even know if he was supposed to drink while taking chemotherapy drugs, but regardless, Sophie had lured him, enticed him in. She thought they needed to toast his turnaround in fortunes—and as luck would have it, it was also the anniversary of their meeting in Detroit, the night of the hockey game in the Joe Louis Arena, so the reasons to celebrate were two-fold. The fact that his friend remembered this date every year amazed Ethan—but then, she had a freakish memory, capable of easily recalling birthdays, anniversaries, and other momentous moments in the lives of her incredibly wide circle of friends.

It was a Saturday night and they had originally planned to cook in, but instead they walked a few blocks to the Thirsty Marlin, where they got an outside table and Sophie ordered two big margaritas. She was in a strange mood: elated because the assembly was on the horizon and Ethan was coming, but melancholy, too. It took a few drinks before the underlying issues came out and she told her friend she had been feeling depressed about her own sexuality and the absence of a relationship.

Sophie feeling sad about love came as a complete shock to Ethan, and immediately made him feel selfish. She wasn't angry or depressed, but melancholy in a thoughtful way, with some of the feelings growing out of his own pursuit of a soul mate. This gave him a reason to try to match her drinking. He felt guilty—guilty that his own emotional turmoil had affected her, but also because his illness and the time Sophie had spent helping him might have impacted her ability to form a meaningful relationship elsewhere.

Sophie had been listening to her friend over the past few months. She had been as thoughtful in the movie *50-50* as he had been, had rented *Good Will Hunting* to refresh her memory of the storyline and to listen to the quote that Ethan had given her, the question that had been posed to Will about his soul mate. She had been walking down the same emotional road as her friend—quietly and a few steps behind.

For a while, as Ethan watched her sift through emotional thoughts, he continued to feel at fault. But that feeling faded as the alcohol kicked in and as Sophie talked and cried. He found himself at last in a position to be a friend, to listen and support, to empathize and to be there as she followed a process that eventually led to a moment of calm.

"Thank you, Ethan. I'll be okay. I'm just feeling sorry for myself. I am a good person, doing good things with my life, helping others. I need to have faith, like you have faith."

Three margaritas into the evening, the conversation turned around, focused back on Ethan. Sophie, it seemed, was fascinated with what she saw as his metamorphosis. She felt cancer had really changed him, and after the initial stages, when his level of defeatism had dismayed her, she felt he had become a new person—or at least, a potentially new person.

"Don't forget, Sophie, it was your insistence that I change, that I open up to myself and others. The thoughtful conversation that you initiated in the coffee shop made me feel and act differently."

Ethan, fueled by tequila, speculated that he was like a seedling in the desert, one of those deserts that were shown on Animal Planet or The Nature Channel: dry and barren for several years in a row until the rains came, and then suddenly, full of greenery and color, with life where before there had been dry, gritty sand. The household in which he'd grown up; the tough school he'd attended; the coarse, concrete city through which he'd wandered in his formative years; the sterile setting that was his workplace, all frowns and desks and numbers—he had not found an environment conducive to love, until cancer had shown him one.

At that point, Ethan had stopped drinking, but Sophie had a fourth margarita, and that was when she asked her friend what he was going to do when he got to Austin. He said he was going to do nothing, and explained that the LIVE**STRONG** Foundation was funding Sophie's program and he was not going to do anything to jeopardize that.

Ethan's reasoning made no difference to Sophie. She saw the assembly as a symbol, the personification of her friend's battle against cancer and his effort to be who he really was. If he did nothing—just observed this symbol and left—she was afraid that the whole effort, the whole reason he was attending the assembly, would be for nothing—pointless.

She then smiled and asked if her friend had heard who the keynote speaker was going to be in Austin. When he shook his head, she told him. Calvin Carter had been a wide receiver at Michigan, on the same team as Tom Brady, and now played for the Detroit Lions. He had survived a bout of testicular cancer in his mid-twenties and was coming to the assembly to tell his story.

At that time, at that table, as Ethan sat in cool night air tinged with a pleasant sea breeze, another fateful sign had appeared—and Sophie made sense. He did not want this once-in-a-lifetime opportunity to be wasted—so Ethan wrote a letter to Calvin Carter.

He was not drunk enough to even think that he would approach the man himself in front of hundreds of people, but he was drunk enough to decide to let him know on paper what he was feeling and what he was trying to achieve. On an off-white piece of paper with the Thirsty Marlin logo and address at the top, he wrote:

Dear Calvin,

*I am a cancer survivor battling adrenal cortical carcinoma. Like many other cancer survivors, I have been helped and inspired by the LIVE**STRONG** Foundation. I will be attending the upcoming assembly because I am a participant in the LIVE**STRONG** at the YMCA program—attending physically at their invitation, but also spiritually and emotionally because of the gift of life they have given to me. You are a survivor, Calvin. You understand the depth of emotion that comes when a helping hand and hope appears in the depth of despair. To say I feel gratitude toward the LIVE**STRONG** Foundation is not enough—I feel love.*

I am also an athlete, like you. Perhaps that is a little bold of me—to compare myself to a world-class wide receiver in the NFL. But I'm feeling bold. I am relaxing with my best friend, drinking margaritas and writing to a superstar, and in a few weeks I am going to visit a doctor to hear if I am a victim or a victor—defeating or succumbing to cancer.

I am an amateur cyclist, a very limited amateur cyclist, but someone who loves the freedom that surrounds a bike and the rider on that bike, who loves the simplicity of the activity and the sense of liberation that comes when speed and power are provided to the slow and weak. As a cyclist, I have an escape, can use the rush of blood and adrenaline on a ride to turn me into an elite athlete, to pull me up and down the steep hills of my cancer journey.

*So since I am writing to a fellow athlete and fellow survivor, and I'm feeling bold, why shouldn't I be as open and honest as possible? Calvin, I am a man with a secret, and cancer has provided me with the motivation to reveal that secret. I am gay, beginning to feel okay with being gay, hoping soon to be proud that I am gay. There is no real reason that I am revealing this to you, other than to be able to say to myself that two people in the world know that I am gay: my best friend and a highly paid professional athlete who cares enough to speak at a LIVE**STRONG** Foundation event, to inspire other survivors and give them hope.*

I am very much looking forward to the assembly. To be able to represent the **LIVESTRONG** *at the YMCA program, which has saved me in more ways than one, will be special. I hope to be able to see you and say hello.*

Love, health and many thanks for all that you do.

Ethan Clarke

Sophie had read the letter, cried, and then asked Ethan to talk to her, to make her feel needed. The two friends hugged, and Ethan had whispered in her ear all the things she meant to him, a list of adjectives and superlatives that outlined how much he loved her.

In response, to return that love in kind, she had looked up the address of the **LIVESTRONG** Foundation in Texas on her phone, found a stamp in her purse, cajoled the owner of the Thirsty Marlin into giving her an envelope—and on the way back to the house, the letter was mailed.

There was a moment when the enormity of what he had done threatened to sink in, but then Sophie had pulled Ethan away from the mailbox and laughed, telling him that she had decided to stay the night and did he have any wine?—and they had staggered away, forgetting and remembering together.

27

If he had been nervous on the plane, it was in Austin that the potential consequences of Ethan's letter really sank in. It was just one of many reasons to feel anxious. The nerves stayed with him as he traveled to the hotel and conference center, checked into his room, and prepared to immerse himself in the event. He took time to breathe, to try to focus on other things—and then he left his room to begin to live the dream.

When he made it downstairs to join the gathering of YMCA staff, he found Sophie working a room of about fifty people, with others still arriving. He could tell she was overjoyed to be face-to-face with individuals she had been e-mailing and calling all year. She had an animated expression, with big smiles, handshakes, and hugs for everyone she met.

She eventually spotted Ethan over to the side, as he glanced over the final agenda and tried to look inconspicuous so as not to spoil any reunions for his friend. Sophie called to him, waving him into the center of the room to be introduced to key staff members that she worked with around the country. All of the individuals were genuine with their greetings, and all knew Ethan by name—Sophie had talked about him on calls and in previous meetings. As a group, they asked about his health, his progress, and where he was on his cancer journey, and as a group, they wished him the best with his tests. They were friendly, genuine people, and after the introductions were over, they returned to the business of beginning a conference.

That first afternoon had Ethan in tears—and he wasn't the only emotional person in the room. The gathering had all the energy and focus that he had expected when the focus was LIVE**STRONG** at the YMCA and the impact the initiative was having on cancer survivors around the country. Staff members shared stories, listened, analyzed, and asked questions, making notes so that programs back home could be improved or post-conference connections could be made with experts in another area of the country. Not all of the key individuals involved in LIVE**STRONG** at the YMCA had made it to Austin, mainly because of cost or schedule conflicts, so notes and photos were being taken, handouts collected, and packets put together for friends back home.

For an outsider, the wealth of information shared and the passion and impact embedded in that information made the occasion exhausting; for the staff, on the other hand, the whole process seemed joyous. Sophie and her colleagues worked, mingled, and organized in an electric fashion. The gathering was a blaze of energy because there was so much to do and so little time in which to do it, and the importance of the effort expended here was incalculable.

For dinner, everyone had to decide where they wanted to go and who they wanted to go with; there was nothing planned at the hotel. Austin apparently was the Ann Arbor of the South, except with the University of Texas camped downtown and accents that drawled in a distinctly Western way. Local staff had recommended a variety of restaurants, many featuring Tex-Mex themes and flavors, but Ethan begged off: he was very tired, and he wanted to get to his room to think and type while his emotions were fresh. Hovering in the far reaches of his mind was Fat-Fingered Tony and his offer, but he also thought it might be good for Sophie to relax and catch up with her peers alone, worry-free.

The morning session with the YMCA involved the same staff members that he had been with on the first afternoon, but there was a different format. This time there were true breakout groups that met either in different areas of the very large conference room or in separate rooms altogether. The focus this time was on areas of excellence exhibited in Ys around the country—on program pieces or new initiatives that had been so successful that many of the other Ys wanted to understand and perhaps replicate the work, so that they could share in the success.

The second day hummed by in the same fashion as the first, until, by the next session, Ethan's nerves had returned. There was an hour dedicated to another round of work groups, and then they had the State of the Foundation luncheon to attend. That was when the keynote speaker would appear.

Sophie had talked to Ethan about the 2011 assembly, when there had been a State of the Foundation dinner. Again, it had been held at a high-end hotel, and at the dinner, tables had been filled with community partners and also major donors to the LIVE**STRONG** Foundation. That was clearly one of the reasons for the first assembly: not only to bring together grassroots worker bees who had benefited from foundation funding, but to bring together major donors and put them in the same room with those worker bees.

Sophie felt that it had worked the previous year. It was impressive to staff members from the YMCA and other organizations to see affluent supporters of the foundation. It was even more impressive to be having dinner with these affluent supporters, and it felt like it was important for the donors to be there, too. Seeing so many community members who were working to support cancer survivors and who were grateful for the support that the LIVE**STRONG** Foundation had given them was a reflection on the organization, but was, of course, a reflection on the donors, too, and was hopefully an incentive to give again.

The one moment that had stood out for Sophie from the previous year was Lance's entrance into the room, and she had described the full scenario to Ethan in great detail several times. Like this year, no one had known whether Lance would attend. The 2011 meeting was the first big LIVE**STRONG** Assembly attended by YMCA staff, and around the conference, rumors were rife concerning Lance: Was he in Austin? Was he in the hotel? Was he going to attend the dinner?

He had not been at the head table when everyone came in to sit, although there were some impressive faces, including Dr. Sanjay Gupta, who was a keynote speaker, and Brian Rose, a thirty-two-year-old baseball coach who had been diagnosed with stage four melanoma. But before either speech had begun, as the tables settled and after most of the guests had arrived, in strode a casually dressed individual, in a parka and jeans, no less, and the room erupted. Lance was in the house.

He had spoken briefly, mainly to thank everyone for coming and to introduce the speakers for the night, and then he was at his table, and necks craned and heads turned for the rest of the night. Straight after dinner, with all of the speeches finished, he was gone, as swiftly as he had arrived.

Ethan had no idea if the atmosphere with a different speaker would be similar this year. Of more importance to him was the thought that Calvin Carter may have received his letter—and may have been, in some way, offended by its message. The consequences of his drunkenness affected his ability to focus on the work group sessions, but he tried. One of Sophie's closest friends was presenting a more in-depth piece on exercise and cancer survivorship, but Ethan wanted to broaden his horizons, and so he went to a session on resources for people who were struggling with grief and recovery.

The presentation and discussion were excellent, but he remained distracted, and before the talk was over, he had to get up and leave. The rock in the pit of his stomach had returned, and he had to calm himself before the luncheon. Ethan had reached the stage where he just wanted to get through an ordeal, and any thought of achieving a goal of any kind had disappeared.

He went outside and made a circuit around the hotel, breathing and thinking peaceful thoughts. Eventually, after he sat on a couch in the lobby for a few minutes, one thought allowed him to smile, shake his head, and stand, ready for lunch. It was the thought that he was going to have a scan in a few days' time to determine whether he was close to death or ready for life. Compared to that, did upsetting Calvin Carter really matter? No, it didn't, Ethan decided. He walked over to a stream of people heading eagerly toward the main ballroom, where lunch was being served, and scanned the crowd for Sophie. When he found her, he kissed her on the cheek.

Sophie had insisted on sitting at a table with her friend for the lunch. She felt bad that he had stayed in the previous night while she went out—by all accounts until pretty late at night—even though he told her that he had relaxed and, more importantly, slept. She wanted to see how he was feeling and ask him what he thought of the conference, and she especially wanted to be near Ethan when the special guest appeared.

Everyone walking through the door was being greeted by a group of LIVE**STRONG** Foundation volunteers who told them to sit wherever they wanted, and as they looked around at a rapidly filling room, the noise began to grow. This was Ethan's first exposure to the wider foundation "family," as the staff had called it several times. It was clear that this gathering, this sit-down meal, was different from the one that had occurred the year before. It was still a sumptuous affair served by hotel waiters, but less formal and with no head table full of special guests. Instead, it was open plan, and seats were being filled by volunteers and staff from organizations that were supported by the LIVE**STRONG** Foundation and who worked diligently and passionately to improve the lives of cancer survivors.

A buzz filled the room, similar to the one Ethan had heard in the YMCA session, the hum of energetic, cause-driven individuals, now electrified in the presence of other cause-driven people. There was less concern about where to sit than with whom to sit—many folks had not seen each other for a year, since they worked in communities on different sides of the country and only came together when the foundation called. Friends were reconnecting left and right, with handshakes, hugs, and hoots of delight.

Ethan and Sophie were joined at their table by young adults from an organization called Camp Kesem. The half dozen people they sat with were teens and college students: extremely mature and responsible young men and women who introduced themselves right away, explained their organization, and then immediately asked insightful questions about the Y and what the Y did to help survivors. Camp Kesem provided week-long summer getaways for the children of cancer survivors, and was staffed and funded entirely by these students. One volunteer at the table, Bethany, explained that *kesem* meant "magic" in Hebrew—and as the food was served, the descriptions they gave of the children in the program and the activities at the camp explained the use of the name perfectly.

So many organizations were represented at this gathering: patient navigators, fertility advisors, promoters, and LIVE**STRONG** leaders. The hum of engagement increased as individuals and groups enjoyed their lunch, conversed, and swapped stories until, just as the buzz was about to reach a crescendo, it changed to rapturous applause. Doug Ulman, the president and CEO of the LIVE**STRONG** Foundation, had walked onstage.

The Camp Kesem ladies were incredibly excited to see Doug Ulman, and everyone in the room was on their feet to recognize a truly inspirational leader. Ethan found himself standing up, too. The electricity was flowing; it was a special occasion, with special people who were helping people like him. It was not a time to feel nervous, but a time to feel appreciative and excited. As the CEO began his speech, Ethan relaxed with a big sigh.

Doug Ulman was a unique individual, although, like many of the staff in the room, he would not have described himself that way. He was a three-time cancer survivor who had made it through melanoma and bone cancer treatments—three separate cases between his nineteenth and twentieth birthdays. He again provided perspective on what Ethan was going through, but also continued a tone and theme that he had heard and sensed throughout his time in Austin: Ulman was humble, not at all focused on himself, but rather focused on the gathered group of leaders and the work they were doing.

His speech lasted about twenty minutes, during which he said thank you about twenty times to a room that was silent and respectful. He outlined how important the gathered volunteers and organizations were to the LIVE**STRONG** Foundation, explained what many of the groups were doing, and emphasized, as Sophie had said he would, that his organization did not want to grow and spread and become the biggest and best, but wanted to support others so that *they* could grow and spread. As he talked, Ethan listened, looked around the room, and thought how personally empowering the trip had been. Even before the second day was over, it had been successful for him, and clearly for many others as well.

As Doug Ulman was wrapping up, the tone of his voice and the subject matter changed. Ethan had not been paying attention as he looked around the room at faces of different ages and colors, of women and men. But when the speaker began to refer to the history of the LIVE**STRONG** Foundation and the many friends and supporters the organization had, a very muted version of the earlier buzz began around the room. Sophie looked at Ethan, and his heart skipped a beat. "Please welcome our very special guest, Calvin Carter."

Everyone was standing; those close to the front scurried forward, and cameras clicked and flashes popped. A genuine star was in the room, and so much happiness had followed him. It was amazing the effect he had, the aura. He may not have been the creator of the foundation, but he was a highly successful athlete who had survived cancer.

Ethan turned his gaze from the stage and Calvin Carter for a moment and looked around the room—and saw on the faces of his companions not only respect and admiration, but also genuine love for the man onstage. This man meant something more than the cancer, football, and fame. Sophie had said it was pure hope—and perhaps it was.

Ethan tried to take in everything that was said, but he couldn't. He was in an emotional and reflective daze, and he looked back around the room and at Sophie as much as he looked at the man on stage. His friend was a wise woman.

As he sat in a location that seemed to be fundamentally changing his own cancer and life journey, Ethan was replaying in his head the tough talk that had been the original catalyst for his change. Sophie had covertly targeted his selfishness that day in the coffee shop, and she had been right. He was sitting in a room full of people, listening to speeches from great men, and all present affirmed her point of view. For Ethan, his own cancer journey needed to be less about Ethan. Cancer was going to do what cancer was going to do, and of course he needed to fight like hell—but he also needed to be respectful enough of himself and his experiences to know that he could help others, and in doing that, be helped in return.

He thought about all his sporting analogies and understood that he was using the wrong clichés. There were others more appropriate, like "It's not about winning, it's about playing the game," or "Everyone plays and everyone wins." For many **LIVESTRONG** Foundation supporters, it seemed to be about surviving, without a doubt; but also about how they survived, and, if it came to it, how they died. The manner of survivorship was all-important. If Ethan had felt his eyes being pried open by Sophie and her anger in the coffee shop, in Austin he felt his heart being pried open, and it was like a religious experience.

Then, as the room stood in unison again and Calvin Carter said his farewells in words and waves, the experience was compounded. It looked like volunteers and ushers were waiting for both speakers to exit stage left, and that was where Doug Ulman walked. But the big wide receiver paused, and then headed the opposite way. As the Camp Kesem girls stared in awe, he skipped down off the stage, walked around the table and held out his hand to Ethan. As they shook, he leaned in close.

"I got your letter, Ethan, and it meant a lot. Good luck with the tests. I'll be thinking of you."

And then, with a smile and a nod, he was gone.

28

It was a day of celebration and reflection when Ethan found out his tests were negative and he was cancer-free—for the time being, at least. He met with a different oncologist and she was very straightforward and honest. She said it could have been that his medication worked and the chemotherapy killed all of the cancer present in his body; he had certainly been taking a powerful dose of the drug. She also said that it was possible the set of tests after his operation had been falsely positive. She said that a remarkably high number of computerized scans for cancer came back with false positives and that it was unfortunate, but that it was also something the scientific community was trying to address. She told Ethan that he was likely to be on the oral chemo for a long time, perhaps for the rest of his life, because of the type of cancer he had had, but that the levels of the drug would be lowered gradually. Apparently adrenal cancer was very virulent, and since he had had one rogue cell that had become cancerous, they wanted to make sure he didn't have another.

There was a hint of trepidation in the doctor's voice as she passed on the news that his first set of scans after the surgery might have been wrong, as though even the possibility of a false positive in the past had led to anger alongside relief. But Ethan really didn't care why the test had been positive in the first place—he cared only that it was negative now. He shook the oncologist's hand in a very formal way as he was about to leave—but then shrugged and asked if he could hug her, which made her laugh.

Sophie was in a board meeting and hadn't been able to come with her friend, but she had made him promise to text her when he got the news. She told him later that she had screamed out loud in the middle of the financial report, which had shocked her volunteers into silence. The reason for the scream made up for everything, but Ethan wondered what her reaction would have been if he had texted her bad news.

After Sophie, his next call was to Dave, who laughed in a relieved way and promised to meet at the Y the next day to exercise and talk.

Ethan was happy that he had reconnected with Dave—it had been a goal of his ever since his friend's son had died. The first thing he had done when he returned from Austin, after a good night's sleep, was call up members of his LIVE**STRONG** at the YMCA group to ask them if they would come with him to visit Dave and Mary that evening. He felt like he really wanted to share the Austin experience with his cancer survivor friends, and with Dave in particular. Brenda and Steve had been able to make it, and Dave and Mary were very happy to entertain them, to let them know how they were and to share in the excitement that Ethan couldn't keep inside as he talked about the assembly.

After he had made a few more calls to his family to share the test results, he spent a few hours just wallowing in a feeling of relief, and then went out to celebrate with Sophie. They ate at Frenchy's, a classic tourist bar and restaurant right on Clearwater Beach, and when they finished eating, they walked down onto the sand and Sophie sat wrapped in her friend's arms as the sun went down. It was unseasonably cool for April and therefore quiet on the beach. What was probably the last cold snap of the year was moving over them and off to the east.

It was a contented scene, with both friends having good reason to enjoy the solitude and silence. Sophie felt relaxed and relieved that the assembly was over and her friend was well—and Ethan's mind was free of turmoil for the first time in months, maybe years. Unfortunately, he had to change the mood—there were things to say.

Gently and quietly, he mentioned he was thinking about leaving his job, to spend some time with his mom and then to move up to New York, to meet with Tony and see if he could start a writing career of some kind.

Sophie squeezed his arms tight and cried. She then said that perhaps, eventually, she would follow him again, and that he should look out for job openings at the Y.

After he had driven home, Ethan was still restless, so he told Jay to jump in the car and they went down to the Dunedin Causeway. It was unusually quiet because it was so cold, and also late, so he parked in a lot next to a kayak rental shop, facing the sea with the headlights on. When Ethan opened the car door, Jay immediately raced off toward the sea, barking excitedly and scattering seagulls into the air. Ethan followed and sat cross-legged in the sand to watch his dog challenge the waves by skipping fearlessly down as they retreated, then turning and racing up the beach as the water rushed back toward him.

Ethan was not thinking about cancer, but he was thinking about the card that had come in the mail that morning, just before he left for the doctor's office to get his test results. It was perfect timing, and if he was being honest with himself, he had known that he was cancer-free as soon as it arrived. He could not possibly have received a card from Calvin Carter in the mail and then been told he had cancer. It was short and sweet: "Good luck, buddy, thinking of you," in a muscular scrawl—but it was so nice that he had thought to do that. Who was Ethan, after all—just another brother in a family of survivors that numbered in the hundreds of thousands.

The best thing about briefly meeting this famous athlete in Austin, and then his card, was that Ethan's sexuality didn't seem to be a problem for the man. He had made an effort to reach out after his talk at the assembly because Ethan was a cancer survivor who had written a letter. He had sent a card back because he had decided to do so—to help fellow survivors regardless of race, politics, or sexual orientation. It was the person who mattered, the cancer that mattered.

The next day, Ethan was going to reveal his secret to his **LIVESTRONG** at the YMCA group. He planned to show them his card, and then be quick and honest: "My friends, I am gay. How do you feel about that?"

Then he was going to call his editor friend and formally take him up on his offer. He was going to write for Fat-Fingered Tony—and he was so excited!

A LIVE**STRONG** at the YMCA participant, 2010

Not all cancer miracles occur in the operating room. Three months ago, I arrived at the Y a shadow of the person I had been just a year earlier. Cancer had not only robbed me of many aspects of my physical identity, it had taken away so much of my confidence, my energy . . . , my *joie de vivre*. By all medical accounts my health was on the mend, but my body and my spirit remained, if not broken, certainly compromised. A year after my diagnosis, ten months after surgery and four months since my last radiation treatment, I was beginning to wonder whether this constant state of lifelessness was just something I was just going to have to get used to.

I was broken in ways that neither doctors, nor friends, nor family could repair. And I wasn't alone.

When a friend of mine who works at the Y asked me if I'd heard of LIVE**STRONG** at the YMCA, I was intrigued enough to look into it. Thank goodness I did. As my twelve weeks in this program wind down, I can reflect upon it as a symbol of hope and redemption in my own personal cancer experience. Today I have muscles where I've never had muscles before. I can run five miles. I've lost fifteen pounds. More importantly, LIVE**STRONG** at the YMCA has shown me—and each and every one of my lovely, able, and courageous classmates—that despite everything we've gone through and everything that's been lost to us, we are stronger than we think we are, and we each have a lot more fight left in us than perhaps we realized. Most of us don't expect to come out the other side of our cancer experience stronger and happier than we were when we went in. And, sadly, not all of us will.

But my classmates and I are living, breathing, thriving proof that with the right kind of encouragement from dedicated, caring professionals like Suzanne, Marie, Mary Beth, and Maureen, the end of the cancer experience can be the beginning of the fittest and happiest chapter of our lives.

Author's Note

~

I first came to America in the mid-nineties as an English YMCA staff member with a goal—to deepen my understanding of an organization that had a presence in 120 countries around the world and had been in existence for over 150 years. I unpacked my bags for the first time in the States on the top floor of the old downtown Detroit YMCA, and one month later, I moved to the Ann Arbor Y, into a room that was my home for over a year. Immersing myself so thoroughly in the Y culture—living with residents, working with staff, eating, recreating, exploring streets and districts—helped me fall in love with two very different but equally historic and celebrated communities.

The YMCA no longer has housing in either city. Other, better-equipped civic groups now provide shelter for those in need. But both organizations have kept a downtown presence, building state-of-the-art branches that showcase the Y's status as a leading provider of programs that focus on health, wellness, and youth development. Along with activities that they are traditionally strong in—group exercise, individual exercise, youth sports, swim lessons, camping, and teen programming—the YMCAs in Detroit and Ann Arbor make a point to help in other areas of need. So, in Ann Arbor, the Y has developed a Youth Volunteer Corps, which involves hundreds of teens collaborating with other charities and county agencies to serve people in need; and Chain of Plenty, a program that helps high school students with special needs gain job and life skills as they prepare meals for the homeless. In Detroit the focus has been on education, so the YMCA Service Learning Academy was born, serving over 1,100 kindergarten through eighth-grade students in the northwest part of the city. It was soon followed by the YMCA Leadership Academy, serving over 300 elementary school-aged children in Brightmoor.

After Michigan, and after I had spent a year in Africa, I began working for the YMCA of the Suncoast, an extremely progressive organization. The Suncoast YMCA was one of the first Ys in the country to develop a comprehensive method for collecting hard facts—data that could outline how impactful the Y was in communities, and help the Y improve the services it offered to individuals and families with a variety of needs. As this story highlights, Suncoast was one of the initial ten YMCAs that helped to develop the LIVE**STRONG** at the YMCA program, and I was lucky enough to be chosen as the project manager leading that charge. I was lucky because I witnessed at close hand the birth of a tremendously impactful program, and because I came into contact for the first time with the LIVE**STRONG** Foundation, an organization with as much of a focus on mission as the Y.

The mission emphasis inspired me to make sure that all of the author royalties from this book are used to help sustain cause-driven programs in communities around the country. Royalties generated from the sale of *A Love Letter* will be donated to the LIVE**STRONG** Foundation and its support of LIVE**STRONG** at the YMCA, and 50 percent of these donated funds will be used to help local Y programs through a grant-making process called the "Impact and Inclusion Awards." Brandylane Publishers is also donating 5 percent of its net proceeds to the LIVE**STRONG** Foundation.

For more information on the awards, or for any questions about this book, feel free to contact me at ymcabrit@icloud.com.

Afterword

~

This book takes place over a period of time when the true extent of Lance Armstrong's involvement with performance-enhancing drugs was not known. That picture is clearer now—but for many cancer survivors, ambivalence reigns. Few condone cheating, but many remember the example set by Armstrong as a cancer survivor and the efforts he made as an individual to reach out to and support individuals affected by the disease.

While this book touches on the aura of Lance, it also highlights the amazing impact the LIVE**STRONG** Foundation has had on the lives of cancer survivors around the country and around the world. For various reasons, it is important to remember that Lance Armstrong is no longer a part of that organization. The LIVE**STRONG** Foundation is a very effective agency providing vital support to individuals and organizations in the cancer community. We are pleased to put a percentage of the proceeds from this book toward the work carried out by this wonderful organization.

Appendix

~

About LIVE**STRONG** at the YMCA

T he Y and the LIVE**STRONG**® Foundation joined together to create LIVE**STRONG** at the YMCA, a physical activity and well-being program designed to help adult cancer survivors achieve their holistic health goals. The research-based program offers people affected by cancer a safe, supportive environment to participate in physical and social activities focused on strengthening the whole person. Participants work with Y staff trained in supportive cancer care to achieve their goals, such as building muscle mass and strength; increasing flexibility and endurance; and improving confidence and self-esteem. In addition to physical benefits, LIVE**STRONG** at the YMCA focuses on the emotional well-being of survivors and their families by providing a supportive community where people impacted by cancer can connect during treatment and beyond. By focusing on the whole person and not the disease, LIVE**STRONG** at the YMCA helps people move beyond cancer in spirit, mind and body. For more information about the program or to find a location, visit www.LIVE**STRONG**.org/YMCA.

About the LIVE**STRONG** Foundation

The LIVE**STRONG** Foundation fights to improve the lives of people affected by cancer *now*. Created in 1997, the foundation is known for leading an ongoing dialogue with patients and survivors, providing free cancer support services and advocating for policies that improve access to care and quality of life. Known for its powerful brand—LIVE**STRONG**—it has become a symbol of hope and inspiration around the world. Since its inception, the foundation has served 2.5 million people affected by the disease and raised more than $500 million to support cancer survivors. One of America's top non-profit organizations, it enjoys a four-star rating from Charity Navigator and has been recognized by the National Health Council and the Better Business Bureau for its excellent governance, high standards and transparency. For more information, visit LIVE**STRONG**.org.

©LIVE**STRONG**, a registered trademark of the LIVE**STRONG** Foundation

Mike Roberts was a semi-pro soccer player and part-time coach in England until he discovered the mission of the YMCA. He began his new career in London, encouraging homeless young men and women to become active and exercise before he moved to Ann Arbor, Michigan to develop a youth sports and camp program. After spending a year with the Y in Zimbabwe, he joined the YMCA of the Suncoast in Clearwater, Florida, where he became a project manager, helping to develop LIVE**STRONG** at the YMCA, an exercise program for cancer survivors. Mike is now an Executive Director in Petersburg, Virginia and helps to spread LIVE**STRONG** at the YMCA to new Y's around the country.